The look Sie sent him over

It was pure sexual

"Sorry, I'm a little edgy," Sierra admitted. "But I'm only that way when I have some huge, irritating guy following me around all day."

"So you remember me as huge, huh?" Reece asked wickedly, referring aloud for the first time to their little encounter at the resort. Up-against-the-wall, no-holds-barred sex that had kept him awake many nights since.

Heat, fast and intense, flashed in her blue eyes. The look, brief though it was, assured him that nothing about their closet encounter had slipped her mind. And, thank God, the swift glance she slid to his zipper guaranteed those moans of pleasure he'd tortured himself with nightly had been the real deal.

"A huge pain in the butt, yes," she said.

She was driving him nuts. All he cared about was tasting her, proving to himself that his memories were real.

"Didn't your momma ever warn you about riling a horny bull, sweetheart?" he asked, pulling her close. Then, giving her no time for the smart comeback he knew she'd deliver, he covered her lips with his.

Available in September 2010 from Mills & Boon® Blaze®

CAUGHT ON CAMERA

BY
TAWNY WEBER

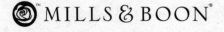

First published in Great Britain 2010
Harlequin Mills & Boon Limited,
Eton House, 18-24 Paradise Road, Richmond, Surrey TW9 1SR

Caught on Camera © Tawny Weber 2009
(Original title *Going Down Hard*)

ISBN: 978 0 263 88144 8

14-0910

Harlequin Mills & Boon policy is to use papers that are natural, renewable
and recyclable products and made from wood grown in sustainable forests.
The logging and manufacturing processes conform to the legal environmental
regulations of the country of origin.

Printed and bound in Spain
by Litografia Rosés S.A., Barcelona

Tawny Weber is usually found dreaming up stories in her California home, surrounded by dogs, cats and kids. When she's not writing hot, spicy stories for Blaze®, she's testing her latest margarita recipe, shopping for the perfect pair of boots or drooling over Johnny Depp pictures (when her husband isn't looking, of course). When she's not doing any of that, she spends her time scrapbooking and playing in the garden. She'd love to hear from readers, so drop by her home on the web, www.TawnyWeber.com.

To The Romance Bandits:
Jeanne, Beth, FoAnna, Kate, Caren, Kim,
Joan, Christie, Jo, Donna, Cindy, Trish,
Cassandra, Nancy, Kristen, Susan,
Vrai Anna, Christine & Suz!

You all rock!

1

IT WASN'T EVERY DAY a woman got to see her naked self coated in chocolate and being licked like an ice cream cone by a dozen people. Apparently hot fudge was the syrup of choice for an orgy.

Cringing, Sierra Donovan peered at the grainy black-and-white eight-by-ten photo starring her and her twelve new best friends. Struggling to be objective instead of giving in to the terror taking hold in her belly, she forced herself to consider whether the pile of naked bodies was supposed to be sexy.

She was no orgy expert, but wouldn't it be a little hard to get off when you had no idea who was groping what? Cellophane crinkled loudly in the silence as she clenched another piece of candy in her fingers. Unable to deny herself the sugary comfort, she unwrapped the butterscotch sweet and popped it in her mouth as she squinted at the picture. Which body was supposed to be hers? Was she the one between the three guys or was she holding the dripping spoon in her hand?

"Sierra, have you got a second?"

She managed to stifle her scream by crunching down on the butterscotch candy. But she couldn't stop her heart from pounding so hard it had to be stretching her bra strap. Coughing a little, Sierra tossed the picture into her desk drawer and slammed it shut. Giving her best friend a stiff smile she tried to pretend she wasn't having a total freak-out. "Sure," she said. "What do you need?"

Belle Forsham was Sierra's partner in Eventfully Yours, the premier event planning company in Southern California. She was also one hell of a savvy lady. She took one look at Sierra's cheesy smile, hands clasped schoolgirl-perfect on the desk, and the pile of candy wrappers overflowing the trash can. Then she raised a platinum brow and sauntered over to the desk, tucking the files she carried under one arm.

"Give," she said, holding out her hand.

"Have I told you lately how great that rock looks?" Sierra said to stall answering and gestured to Belle's sparkling new engagement ring.

"It is gorgeous, isn't it?" Belle agreed with a sappy smile, taking a second to splay her fingers in order to catch the light with her diamond. If Sierra wasn't a total cynic, she'd have been a smidge envious of her friend's happiness.

But envy was pointless. Besides, finding long-term romantic happiness was as rare as being hit by lightning. In Belle's case, she'd missed out the first time around, then freakishly had a second chance. Belle and the man she'd left at the altar six years ago were now basking in the glow of happy-ever-after.

It gave Sierra a warm, cuddly feeling. Which was bizarre, since she was definitely not a warm, cuddly type of gal. But for her best friend? She'd take up knitting sweaters for teddy bears to prove her happiness.

Belle sat in the cushy chair on the other side of Sierra's cherrywood desk and tucked the files next to her. Kicking off her Jimmy Choos, she curled her feet under her and settled back like she was ready to chat.

The rock-hard tension in Sierra's neck and shoulders eased just a little. Whew, the distraction with the ring had worked. Sure, they'd probably have to talk wedding plans now, but Sierra's forte was planning fancy events so that wasn't much of a hardship. She held back on the sigh of relief, though. No point tipping Belle off.

"I've changed my mind from pastels for the bridesmaids to jewel tones," Belle mused, excitement clear on her doll-like face. "I think you'll look great in sapphire or amethyst silk." Even though the wedding was only three months away, she was still changing things around daily. She arched a brow. "Of course, you look good in anything. Or nothing. I take it you're naked in this picture, too?"

Sierra blinked twice. Then she sighed. So much for distraction.

"Does it matter? So some idiot got their hands on a photo editing program. Obviously they need a lot of practice. Yesterday my head was on sideways, remember?"

The photos, all sexually explicit, all poorly composed with Sierra's face pasted in, had started arriving two months ago. At first, when only one a week showed up, she'd hidden them from Belle since her partner was dealing with a big job and even bigger romance. But for the past two weeks they'd been coming daily. And the perv behind them was getting good enough with photo editing that the photos were starting to make Sierra queasy. Orgies were bad enough, but yesterday's picture had involved farm animals.

Today he'd added commentary.

Soon everyone will know there's nothing sweet about you, was digitally typed over the image.

She was terrified.

But she wasn't about to admit it. Not even to Belle. Nope, Tough Girl 101. To maintain control, all vulnerability had to be hidden. Even if these stupid pictures were to blame for her new two-tube-a-week concealer habit to hide the dark circles brought on from sleep deprivation.

"Give," Belle demanded.

With a grimace Sierra yanked open her drawer and tossed the eight-by-ten across the desk. She watched the glossy paper slide toward her friend, the image even more bizarre upside down.

"Oh my…" Belle's lips moved as she silently counted. "Twelve at once? How do they keep from getting squished, do you think?"

"Good lower body strength," Sierra deadpanned.

Not wanting to watch Belle analyze the creepy picture, Sierra flicked her mouse to take her laptop out of hibernation. Pretending the words weren't blurred and shaky, she tried to focus on her Outlook schedule. They had three events scheduled this week. Two birthday celebrations and a store opening on Rodeo Drive. A signing meeting with a publisher determined to launch with a bang and a pile of billing to get out. Her favorite outlet store would get a delivery of basics on Wednesday, too. With this many events, she needed to keep up appearances, and for her that meant scouring sales. Busy, busy.

She blinked and let the jobs run through her head, the details calming her like no platitudes or assurances could. This she could control. And control was primary for Sierra. Ambitious, outspoken and self-confident, she knew she was damned good at what she did. Her gaze slipped over to Belle's perusal of the latest pervy pic and she clenched her jaw.

These pictures weren't something she could control, though. And they were fast spinning from a minor irritation into a major source of anxiety. If she wasn't careful, she'd end up having panic attacks.

"Sierra, we need to take these to the police."

Yep, there it was. Panic. Sierra's vision blurred to black around the edges, and she felt her heart sprint into high gear. No. She wasn't doing this. Two deep, calming breaths while she focused on her wiggling toes, lovingly encased in the prized pair of red suede Manolos she'd scrimped and saved for eight months to buy. That helped her push away the fear.

"No. This is just some dumbass perv playing games, Belle. I'm not giving him the satisfaction of running to the cops."

"This isn't a game," Belle insisted. "There's a motive behind it. Someone is going to a lot of trouble to terrorize you. Now they're adding threats."

"Commentary," Sierra contradicted, as if it didn't matter. "Look, it's probably just one of our competitors trying to shake us up, you know? He'd have started on you except you have that hottie fiancé you're busy keeping company with."

They both knew that was a slim possibility. The pictures had started to arrive before Belle hooked up with Mitch. While she'd been working on his account, as a matter of fact.

Belle didn't call her on it, though. She just gave Sierra a long, considering look. "How do you know the perv's a he?"

Sierra sneered and poked her finger at the picture still in Belle's hand. "Look at the size of those boobs. Not anything under a C cup there. Totally guy-fantasy crap."

"I agree that it's probably the competition," Belle said. "We're taking over Southern California and kicking ass." Then she tilted her head and added, "But *he* is getting serious. These pictures are coming daily."

Sierra shrugged, trying to blow off the concern. She couldn't, though. Not all of it. After all, just knowing Belle cared enough to worry about her meant she owed it to her friend to do whatever it took to assuage those fears.

"Serious or not," Sierra said, "I'm not letting some freak push me around. What am I supposed to tell the cops, anyway? That someone is sending me dirty pictures? And now he's added captions?"

They'd probably say it was an ex-lover trying to get some kind of revenge. And since she was a healthy twenty-seven-year-old woman, she had a nice list of ex-lovers to choose from. None were stupid or tasteless enough to pull a stunt like this, though. After all, she prided herself in being extremely selective about who she let into her life. Or her bed.

"When did you get your hair cut?" Belle asked.

Sierra blinked again. Usually Belle was much better at the tactful subject changes. Telling herself she was glad to move on and not hurt that her best friend had given up so easily, Sierra brushed her fingers over the blunt edges of her sable hair. "Last week. Tuesday, I think."

After years of flat ironing, special shampoos and blow-dries to pamper her long hair, she'd gone for a shoulder-length style that actually worked with her waves. She'd been afraid it would be too casual, but instead it softened her sharp features and added an air of approachability she'd never had before. If it snagged more clients, it worked for her.

"Tuesday?" Belle repeated flatly.

"Right, why? What's the big deal?"

Belle turned the paper so it faced Sierra and tapped one French-tipped nail at her image. "Apparently you blew off dinner at my place to spend this last weekend in a kinky dogpile, then."

Sierra's stomach lurched and breath stuck in her throat. Well, shit. She'd been concentrating so hard on not being concerned, she'd totally overlooked the fact that her orgy debut featured her new hairstyle.

She sucked in her lower lip and tried to find an explanation. But her mind was blank.

"I'm calling the cops," Belle stated adamantly. "This guy is straight up stalking you."

Sierra rubbed a lock of dark hair with her fingers. Before, she'd tried to write the pictures off as irritating and a little obnoxious. She really had figured it was a competitor trying to shake her up. Or, worst-case scenario, a guy with a twisted way of leading up to hitting on her. But now? She didn't know why she was more worried now, but she was.

She should warn Belle it wouldn't matter, though. Cops

never believed her. Especially when it came to anything sexual. It was as if they took one look at her and figured she was a liar. She'd never understood why, either. She didn't dress provocatively, she didn't flirt randomly, and as much as she liked sex, she could hardly be termed promiscuous.

But when she'd been sexually harassed by her uncle? God, how many times had she called the police as a teenager, asking for protection against the nasty man's advances? His creepy comments, his filthy suggestions and offers. His attempts to corner her, to touch her. She'd dodged him as often as possible, and when dodging hadn't been possible…

Well, suffice it to say, the one time he'd actually managed to shove his hand down her top, she'd shoved *him* down the stairs. The cops hadn't thought much of that, either. Believing her aunt's assertion that she was a mouthy brat, troubled by her mother's recent death and acting out, they'd arrested her for assault. Sierra *had* been troubled, heartbroken to lose her beloved mother at thirteen. But she'd also been so terrified of being abandoned, she'd acted the perfect child when she'd gone to live with her aunt and uncle, despite their accusations to the contrary.

She snatched another candy from the dwindling dish and popped it into her mouth, letting the sweetness coat her tongue, distract her. None of that mattered anymore. All that mattered was that the police weren't going to believe her.

Especially not if they checked her record and saw the accusations her relatives had used in her arrest. Luckily, before she'd died, Sierra's mother had arranged and paid for Sierra to attend a prestigious boarding school starting in ninth grade. The only reason her aunt and uncle had let her escape at fourteen was that it wasn't money out of their pocket, and the possibility that Sierra might blab to the country-club set about her uncle's advances made her even less welcome in their home. Boarding school became her haven. And once she'd met Belle there, her home.

She knew calling the authorities about the photos was useless, but somehow the idea still made her feel as if she were doing something. So she didn't say a word as Belle dialed.

"Okay, the guy I talked to is coming by the office," Belle said as she hung up the phone. "You have all the pictures in a file, right?"

"All there in the drawer," Sierra said, barely concealing her shudder as she unwrapped another piece of candy. If this kept up, she'd put on ten pounds.

Belle glanced at her watch, then grimaced. "I'm supposed to meet the CEO of Family Publications in a half hour to discuss photographers and push her to finally sign this next round of contracts. Let me make a few phone calls and I'll re-arrange the appointment."

Sierra was shaking her head before Belle even finished talking. "No way," she protested. "This picture geek isn't going to upset, change or interfere with Eventfully Yours in any way."

Belle's green eyes rounded at the fierce tone. Her open-mouthed shock made Sierra sigh.

But dammit, she had too much riding on this deal. She'd hooked an account big enough, wide-reaching enough that Eventfully Yours hit it big as a marketing planner as well as an event planning company. But more importantly, the income from this job would make her feel like she'd finally kicked in her part, financially. When they'd started the company five years ago, Belle had fronted the start-up money. She'd never blinked or hinted that she minded, but it still bothered Sierra. After all, Belle was the party girl, Sierra was the organized brain. They each brought a vital element to the business, complementing each other's style and strength. But being able to organize a party for two thousand and arrange seating wasn't enough to pull her weight. Sierra needed to pay her way, too.

All her life, she'd been the rich little poor girl. Wealthy

family, very little money of her own. Fancy boarding school, hand-me-down uniforms. Even now, to keep up with her rich friends and their lifestyle she shopped with coupons, scoured outlet sales and vintage stores.

But now she and Belle were on the verge of hitting it big. Sierra's share of the profits from this new account would pay off her half of the start-up money, provide a tidy little nest egg to invest. And it would buy her the new pair of Louboutins she'd been dreaming about.

But Sierra couldn't tell Belle any of that. Belle would insist, as always, that the money didn't mean anything and brush her off. So Sierra plastered on a calm mask and offered an apologetic smile. "Sorry. It's just that we're on such a great roll lately. Let's just stick with our current plan. I'll handle the cops, you handle the account, okay?"

"Okay," Belle said slowly. She watched Sierra unwrap another candy, this one peppermint, and grimaced. "Look, I know this is upsetting you. I don't think it'll do too much damage if I call to say I'm going to be a little late."

Maybe. Or maybe not. Family was a huge opportunity, one that would add publicity management to Eventfully Yours' prospectus. Instead of planning parties, the business would start handling entire marketing campaigns. For instance, with Family, Sierra and Belle had created a series of events designed to impress the investors and advertisers the publisher was courting. This was their shot to move up, to take on more.

No pervert with a camera was going to ruin it for them.

Figuring she'd break down and cry like a wimp if Belle kept trying to be supportive, Sierra took a deep yoga belly breath and shook her head. "There's no reason for you to stay. The cops will come, look at the pictures, ask a few questions. Besides, this is a key meeting. Even calling to say you're going to be late could jeopardize the power balance."

Most clients were thrilled to let Belle and Sierra call the shots when it came to their events. But some, like this magazine publisher, were heavily into control. Rather than letting her and Belle do their jobs, they were sucking up the gals' time and wasting their own money by demanding approval of every little detail. This meeting to approve the event photographer was a perfect example.

"We want Family to use our people, and they're on the fence already about our photographer because of his last show," Sierra reminded her. The new magazine publisher, a multimedia venture, prided itself on promoting family values. "Tristan might be a little edgy, but he's the best photographer we've worked with and I'd really like to see him on board for this project."

"I think I can swing them around once they see his portfolio," Belle stated. Her green eyes still showed worry, but being a good friend she took her cue from Sierra and focused on business. "But I'll definitely need you there on Monday. This launch is so complicated, they want us both at the next PR meeting."

Sierra nodded, automatically keying the information into her Outlook program.

"Tell you what," Belle said, her words perky and cheerful. Sierra's gaze flew to her friend, and she frowned. What was she up to? "Come by for dinner tonight and we'll compare notes. You can tell me how the cops handled the photos and I'll fill you in on the meeting."

Dinner. It sounded innocent enough, but Belle looked too sweet. Always a bad sign. Since Sierra couldn't think of any reason to refuse, though, she just nodded.

"I'll be by at seven," she agreed. Then as Belle was leaving the room, she added, "Just make sure you're not serving chocolate."

Who knew all it would take to lose her appetite for her favorite sweet was a pile of naked bodies.

Maybe the next shot would include donuts. If so, she'd drop these pesky five pounds in a flash.

THAT EVENING, Sierra smoothed her hand over the silk of her fabulous thrift-store skirt and took a deep, calming breath. Then she rapped on Belle's door.

She'd practiced her breezy smile on the drive over, was sure she had the whole it's-totally-not-a-big-deal verbiage down pat. The last thing she needed was Belle worrying. Or worse, calling the cops again.

Mitch Carter, hottie extraordinaire and Belle's fiancé, let her in with a grin. He had intense brown eyes, a smokin' body and the sweetest smile in the world when he looked at her best friend. If she didn't already think of him as a brother, Sierra would be half in love with the guy. Since half was as far as she ever fell, she figured that said it all.

"Hey, Mitch," she greeted as he welcomed her with a hug. The guy was baffling that way. Über-successful businessman, he was one of the top developers in the country, yet he wore jeans, boots, and gave hugs. As if he didn't have anything to prove. Yup, definitely baffling.

"C'mon in," he said, ushering her through Belle's condo where they were living while their house was being built. Bright and airy with splashes of color, the space suited Belle perfectly. A vivid contrast to Sierra's place with its heavy, dark intensity.

"Yum, homemade guacamole?" she asked as she stepped into the open kitchenette with its long breakfast bar and chrome stools. The red enamel appliances, black-and-white tiled floor and kitschy wall art made the eating area look like a fifties diner gone posh.

Sierra helped herself to a tortilla chip slathered with guacamole, bit it, then saluted her partner with the other half of her chip as she chewed.

"What'd the cops say?" Belle asked from the stove, where she was sautéing onions and bell peppers.

"I'm fine, thanks for asking," Sierra returned with a droll look. "I appreciate the dinner invite—everything smells wonderful. And yes, this is a new skirt. D'ya like it?"

Belle rolled her eyes, but that didn't stop her from dropping her gaze to the vivid red pencil skirt and making an approving noise. But as distractions went, Sierra should have tried shoe shopping, because one second later Belle was raising a brow and giving her that "Well?" look.

Sierra sighed and slipped onto a red vinyl-and-chrome low-backed stool and scooped up more of the avocado dip. She didn't need the seconds it took to eat the chip to gather her thoughts since she'd rehearsed plenty on the drive over, but she used the time anyway.

"The cops said there isn't anything they can do," she reported in a breezy tone as she sipped the margarita Mitch handed her when he walked by.

"They can investigate," Belle insisted, stabbing the vegetables with her spatula.

"Not really. There's no threat. These are just pictures, and pretty crappy ones at that. There is nothing to go on. As offensive as it might be, sending crappy pictures isn't a crime."

Sierra shoved another loaded chip into her mouth to keep the "I told you so" from spilling out next. A shiver of fear worked its way down her spine, but she told herself she hadn't expected anything else. They knew the situation. The cops didn't think it was a big deal.

"But the pictures are blatantly sexual," Belle sputtered in protest.

"No, they are blatantly a joke. Irritating, tacky and rude, but not criminal." At least the police had believed that someone was sending the pictures. They'd been polite, a little surprised at some of the poses, and in one case complimented her on her dexterity. But the bottom line was there was nothing they could do for her. Except offer a grocery list of cautions and warnings, most of which required someone to hold her hand. Just in case.

The idea of a babysitter made Sierra shudder. She totally refused to even consider *just in case*.

"They're going to do something though, right? I mean, they'll keep an eye on you just to make sure you're, you know, safe and all?"

Who knew keeping up a fake smile could be so much work? Just discussing this made Sierra want to scream. But she managed to keep her look cheerful and easygoing. "They wrote up a report. I'll keep them apprised of any more pictures and they'll stay on top of things."

Belle's low growl was a dangerous thing. It wouldn't take much to send her off to the phone to call the cop shop and throw a fit. For a second, Sierra missed the good old days when Belle had backed off from any sort of confrontation.

"When's dinner?" she asked in a blatant subject change. She was done giving those stupid pictures her attention and energy. She'd followed the rules. She'd reported the mess. Now it was time to move on with life. Or more importantly, on to fajitas.

Belle's look was a combination of irritation and something Sierra couldn't quite place. But her friend gave a short jerk of her shoulder, poured the sautéed vegetables on a platter and said, "In a couple minutes. I'm just waiting for Mitch and, um, something."

The something became apparent sixty seconds later when Mitch walked in with a platter of barbecued ribs. Sierra's stomach constricted with sudden nerves, but she didn't know why. Then the scent hit her over the wafting smell of dinner. Earthy, male and totally sexual. Shoulders tight, she turned to watch the man following Mitch.

Her hottest fantasy and her biggest nightmare. The one guy guaranteed to push all her buttons and send every thought of self-preservation straight out of her head.

Temptation in a cowboy hat.

Well, hell, Sierra sighed.

Hadn't her day been stressful enough already?

2

REECE CARTER.

Long, lean and sexy.

Heat flashed in Sierra's belly as she faced the only guy to scare the hell out of her.

Not because he was the sexiest man on Earth and made her want to strip him naked, then lick her way up his body. That she could deal with.

What scared her was that she was a savvy, strong and opinionated woman. But when she saw Reece, she instantly wanted to become sweet, timid and compliant.

So she spent all her time around him being a hard-ass bitch, just to prove she could.

Pathetic.

Her breath quickened as she took in the delicious width of his shoulders encased in a black T-shirt. She wanted to trace her palm over the fabric where it curved lovingly over his big, muscled biceps. She wanted to press her cheek to the hard lines of his torso and run her fingers down the slim, denim-covered hips. The man had a body like a swimmer, with the tightest ass she'd ever seen grace denim.

He made her mouth water.

He had ever since she'd seen him for the first time six years ago at Belle and Mitch's first wedding rehearsal dinner and fallen into instant lust. Then he'd opened his mouth and they'd fallen into instant verbal foreplay. Nobody could turn her on with a few words like Reece could. Unfortunately, nobody could make her lose control with just a few words like he could, either. Because it hadn't taken more than a half-dozen exchanges for her to realize he was too much of a threat to her. To her independence, to her self-control. That hadn't stopped her from getting hot and wild with him on the dance floor, though.

Pitiful that she'd been saved from the biggest mistake of her life when her friend dumped Mitch at the altar. She'd used loyalty as her reason to turn down all of Reece's advances after that. Not that there'd been too many. A few weeks of phone calls, one or two in-person date requests. Then poof, he went away. Just like she'd wanted.

A shame, really. He was so delicious to look at. His white Stetson cast a shadow over wavy black hair, midnight-blue eyes and a chiseled jaw. All-masculine hotness.

Their gazes met. In his eyes she saw both desire and assessment. The unspoken message was that he wanted her like hell, but he didn't like it.

Sierra's shoulders stiffened at the judgment. But that didn't stop her body from going into instant lust mode. For one second, she wished the picture of her face pasted on the woman using the sex swing could be real if Reece was the guy she'd be swinging with.

Then he opened his mouth and, as usual, ruined everything.

"I hear you're doing a little modeling on the side," he teased in his slow, easy drawl.

Telling herself it was fury and not embarrassment she was feeling, Sierra swung around on the stool to glare at Belle. Unrepentant, her friend just shrugged and topped off her half-full margarita. "I thought we could ask Reece what he thought. You know, get a little advice. Maybe some help."

"I don't need help," Sierra claimed, gritting her teeth as she stretched her mouth into a fake smile.

"If you need the police, you need help," Reece said easily.

"I didn't need the police," Sierra returned precisely. She hated that whenever she was around Reece, she felt the need to argue. And win. The need to win was almost overwhelming. But their verbal sparring was like an addictive foreplay. Every time they went up against each other, she got turned on, insanely hot for him. No. Not smart. She needed to stay away from the arguing.

"If you wanted to do a sex pictorial you should have given me a call," Reece said, patting her shoulder to let her know he was teasing. Sierra's first reaction was to pull back so she couldn't feel the heat of his hand on her bare skin. But she wasn't about to give him the satisfaction. Even if the look in his eyes told her he knew.

"There is the one shot with a goat," she returned, determined to hold her own. "It did remind me of you."

"Horny?"

Sierra gave a wicked smile. "Knock-kneed."

Belle gasped, then slapped her hand over her mouth when Sierra glared at her. Mitch, ever the gentleman, mumbled something about checking the barbecue and left.

Reece, though, didn't bother to hide his amusement. His laugh bounced off the walls, his white teeth flashing.

God, did nothing get to the guy? It didn't seem to matter what she said or did, he just came back flirting.

She wanted him to act indifferent. She could handle that. She hated his flirting. It ignited a deep, desperate need inside her to flirt back. But, no. He had to do the one thing that was hardest for her to resist. He was the most frustratingly sexy, irritatingly tempting man she'd ever known.

He worried her even more than the creepy stalker pictures.

"Cops wrote up a report?" He said it as if it were a question, but they all knew it was a statement. Reece was Mr. Security. He'd spent ten years in the army, and while Sierra would rather actually *do* that goat than admit it, the idea of him in his sexy Green Beret uniform had fueled more than one bunny-bout, a term she'd coined in honor of her rabbit-eared vibrator. Now he ran his own security firm.

So he obviously knew his stuff. Which was fine, except Sierra didn't want him mixing his stuff with hers. But—she shot a quick glance at Belle's concerned expression as she scooped black beans into a bowl—she might not get a choice. At least not if she didn't want to worry her best friend.

Caught by the bonds of friendship, Sierra just shrugged and gave Reece a breezy look. "Sure, the police wrote a report. But that was just for form, you know? Poor taste and tacky sex fetishes aren't a crime, as I'm sure you know."

His blue eyes sparkled in wicked delight at her dig. Sierra's lips twitched, but she kept her expression smooth. No point letting him know she was tickled that he'd understood her humor.

"They asked you for a list of suspects?"

"Of course." At his pointed look she rolled her eyes and shrugged. "I have no suspects. If I had a clue who was doing this, I'd go beat them over the head with their own computer."

"Ex-boyfriends, old lovers, new lovers. Guys you've jilted, guys you've scorned, guys you've shot down?"

"Oh yeah, the list was pages long," Sierra said with a wide-eyed expression as she pursed her lips in a way she knew would get his attention. "I was with four different guys last week, but since the Galaxy soccer team is on the road, they figured it wasn't them."

Mitch, who'd just returned, gave a snort of laughter. Reece just shot her a long, considering look. There was something latently violent and predatory in his eyes that made her breath catch. She refused to squirm, though.

Sierra shrugged at Belle's hiss. So what if it was all bullshit. She wasn't going to discuss her sex life with Reece. Duh. She obviously wasn't doing a soccer team. And she wasn't about to admit she hadn't had sex or anything approaching a relationship since she'd slipped up and given in to lust two months ago. Belle had been handling the grand opening of Mitch's resort— their biggest job to date. It had quickly gone from a standard event to a sexfest of planning fun, with a little twist of sabotage. Nobody could say Eventfully Yours didn't go all-out for their clients. In her attempt to distract Reece from discovering Belle sneaking around Mitch's office, Sierra had lost control of her argument with him and they'd ended up doing the nasty.

Just another reason to stay away from him. She never triumphed in their little verbal skirmishes. Even when she won.

The memory of their against-the-wall encounter made her squirm, her silk panties growing uncomfortably warm. Needing to cool off, she grabbed her margarita and drained the deliciously icy concoction in one gulp.

Letting the sugar-laden tequila calm her, she met Reece's eyes with a raised-brow look of her own.

No. He didn't need any encouragement. After all, she knew firsthand how little stroking his…*ego* required to expand to mammoth proportions.

REECE'S FINGERS gripped the neck of his beer bottle so hard it should have shattered. Even though he knew she was giving him a bad time, the idea of any guy's hands on Sierra's body made him crazy. Any guy but himself, of course.

Although from the way the sexy little brunette was glaring daggers at him, he didn't figure he'd be putting his hands on her anytime soon.

He'd never met a woman who challenged him like Sierra did. What baffled him was that she was totally not his type. Reece liked his ladies sweet and biddable. Before ending his disastrous eighteen-month marriage three years ago, he'd pictured himself settling down someday with a sexy little gal who wanted nothing more than to make his life easy, his bed hot and his future kids well-behaved. If that made him an old-fashioned jerk, he was fine with it. He wasn't out to please the world.

He'd spent most of his service years in combat and saw no reason to bring it into his personal life. Or more specifically, his sex life. And yet, Sierra Donovan was the most combative, argumentative, independent woman he'd ever met. And he couldn't get enough of her.

One too many hits to the head, he figured. And he'd get over it, just as soon as he got her out of his system. But he'd come to realize that to do that, he'd have to get her into his bed to work through all the wild fantasies he had.

She was proving a mite uncooperative on that front.

Of course, uncooperative seemed to be Sierra's M.O.

"You gave the cops all these men's names?" he asked, his words featherlight. No point in letting on that she'd got to him. She'd just poke harder if she knew.

"The cops have a full roster of my sexual encounters," she returned with a roll of those pretty blue eyes. "They also have a list of all the people I've pissed off in the last few months."

Her look made it crystal clear he was on both lists.

Reece grinned. Good, he liked being front and center in her mind.

"I'm guessing they didn't plan to follow up," he commented when she was silent.

"Well, they did praise me on my dexterity. And one of them complimented my ability to type with my mouth that full. But like me, they weren't overly impressed with the list itself."

She shoots. She scores.

Reece ground his teeth to hold back his growl of fury. Her offhand comment about the explicit nature of the pictures sparked an angry flame in his gut. He didn't like anger; things always got ugly when he lost his temper. But the implications, the message those pictures were sending, infuriated him.

"The cops have the pictures?" he asked in a matter-of-fact tone.

"They made copies," Sierra admitted with a shrug as she took her empty margarita glass to the sink. Belle handed her a glass of iced tea, the move so easy and natural, he could tell this was their norm.

"But you still have the originals?"

"Why?" she asked, lifting one of the overflowing platters of vegetables from the counter. "Were you looking for something to replace your *Hustler* collection?"

"Well, you have to admit, *Hustler* doesn't feature farm animals."

"And you're such a country boy, you miss that?"

"There ya go," he agreed easily, not bothering to hide his amusement. Taking his cue from her and Belle, who was carrying the bowl of black beans in to dinner, he grabbed the last dish and gestured to the ladies to precede him.

Belle's gaze was shooting back and forth between him and Sierra as if she were following a tennis match. Mitch, though, had his serious CEO look on, which told Reece his cousin was worried. About the stalker pictures or the potential disaster if Sierra cut loose with that temper lurking in her eyes, Reece wasn't sure.

But Sierra didn't say anything. Instead she shot him an unreadable look as she headed toward the dining room.

Was she keeping their hot little encounter a secret from her best friend? Maybe. It'd been two months since they'd had wild closet sex at Mitch's resort and she'd been trying to pretend he didn't exist ever since.

"Let's eat," Belle suggested, obviously trying to break the tension as they all took their seats. "Maybe you can give us some security advice over dinner? Nothing major, just a few ideas on what we can do to deal with this."

From her sigh and the look she shot him, he figured Sierra thought he was a bigger problem than any kinky pictures.

Reece took off his hat, shoved his hand through his hair and made a mental note to get it cut soon. He tossed the hat onto the oak banquette behind him, then took his seat. Belle passed the delicious-smelling platter of fajita fixings to him with a smile. The little blonde was a sweetheart. Perfect for Mitch. Reece hadn't been sure when they'd hooked up again, but now he was. Too bad she'd done the altar dash six years ago, but apparently she and Mitch had both needed time to grow a little.

He sat opposite Sierra and considered the intense brunette. Had she ever been young? When they'd met for the first time, she'd been just as confident, just as cynical and just as sexy as she was now.

Well, he considered, letting his gaze travel over the smooth lines of her bare shoulders and sleek throat, maybe not quite as sexy then. But she definitely had the air of a woman who'd always had her shit together and never struggled with self-esteem issues. He tried to imagine Sierra as a kid or a teenager, but couldn't. Even under an onslaught of dirty pictures, she just didn't come off as vulnerable.

In other words, she was everything his ex-wife had wished to be but never quite pulled off. And Shawna, his classy and ambitious ex, was everything he'd thought he wanted, until he'd realized what he wanted was Sierra, and his ex was just a poor substitute. That flash of insight had come right about the time

Shawna had maxed out his credit cards, sold his car and filed for divorce.

"So," Sierra said as soon as everyone dished up their meal, "why exactly are you here, Reece?"

"The pleasure of your company isn't reason enough?" He piled more spicy salsa on his meat-filled tortilla, hoping nobody would comment if he ignored the vegetables. Belle had that same look in her eye that his grandma got, the kind that said she didn't tolerate slacking when it came to balancing the food groups.

"Belle knows how much I enjoy *your* company," Sierra shot back over her veggie-filled plate, "yet she invited you to dinner anyway."

Reece tipped his head in acknowledgment of the verbal dig. Usually Sierra was smoother. She must be a lot more upset over the picture deal than he'd thought.

And have a lot less respect for his skill than he'd realized. He frowned at the thought. He'd never set much store in other people's opinions, so he couldn't say why that idea bothered him so much. Yet it did.

"I'm guessing the police told you to start keeping the envelopes?" he asked in an even tone as he passed the fajita platter to Mitch. "That if you do open them, to wear gloves so you don't contaminate the evidence. Maybe to take a few personal precautions, make a list of any more names that occur to you. Print up a list of your competitors, note which ones you've outbid for jobs recently. That kind of thing."

Her blue eyes got harder with each sentence. He didn't bother grinning. He just took a big bite of the fajita and waited.

Again, she surprised him. After a quick glance at Belle, Sierra just shrugged and took a vicious bite of her own fajita. Watching her assault the rolled-up tortilla added another image to his dossier of Sierra-inspired sex fantasies.

"Maybe I should step aside for a while," she finally said. For the first time, he saw a hint of fear and worry lining her brow. "If I'm going to jeopardize business, I could work from home. Focus more behind the scenes than out front, you know?"

"Are you bailing on me?" Belle asked.

"No," Sierra snapped.

Reece sat back in his chair and watched her pull herself together. It was fascinating. For a second, her eyes had flared with terror; then they went blank just before she took a breath and closed them. He figured he was the only one at the table who noted her hands were shaking. She didn't even realize it, since he knew she'd have hidden them if she did. After a couple seconds and a quick exchange between Mitch and Belle, who ignored her fiancé's admonishment that she try not to overreact, Sierra opened her eyes and shook her head.

"Look, sweetie," she said, addressing Belle, "I'm not bailing. But I don't want to cause problems, either. I just thought maybe if I stepped back, stayed in the background for a while, it might help. That's all. I don't want him ruining what we've built."

"So you're sure it's a him?" Reece interrupted.

"Sierra figures the photo-happy creep is male because all the pictures feature big boobs," Belle explained with an irritated sniff, shoving her hair off her face as if it were interfering with her ability to wage a winning argument.

Reece bit back a snort of laughter and met Mitch's eyes. His cousin just shrugged and said, "Can't say Belle's not direct."

"She must take tips from Sierra."

The men exchanged amused looks. Belle's lips quirked, but Sierra just rolled her eyes. "Oh please, like you didn't already think it was a guy?"

"The likelihood the stalker is male is high," Reece agreed, the laughter gone from his voice. "If it were a woman, the pictures would be different."

Sierra's derision fell away. A tiny line creased her brow

and he could tell she didn't want to ask, but couldn't help herself. "How so?"

"In a man, you'll see evidence of sexual fantasy, possibly of worship or even signs he wished he could be in the picture, too. In a woman, there would be some element of vindictiveness. Jealousy, catty chick stuff." Agreement flashed in Sierra's eyes, but she didn't do more than tilt her head. He continued anyway. "A woman would have taken the photo editing a little further. You know, made you fat or ugly."

He waited for the explosion, but Sierra only furrowed her brow and gave a little nod of agreement. Reece frowned.

He didn't know which shocked him more—the fact that she'd agreed with something he said, or that she hadn't been pissy about his suggestion she could look bad. In his experience, women didn't like it pointed out that they could ever be less than beautiful. At least, his ex had hated it.

"Well, as fascinating as perverted pictures of me might be, fat or not, I'd much rather hear how the resort is doing. Mitch? What's new in the lives of the decadent?" Sierra's words were smooth and easy, her subject change gracious but resolute. Talk shifted to the luxurious resort where Belle and Mitch had reunited—a playground for the rich and famous that had launched a month and a half ago.

She was done with the stalker talk. Fine with Reece, he was more an action man anyway. As the topic turned to his cousin's resort, he watched Sierra relax into an easy banter of social chitchat.

It wasn't until they'd reached the end of the meal that he realized how skilled she was at the art of meaningless party chatter. She'd talked over and around him, but Sierra never talked directly to him. Oh, she was polite and gracious. The perfect dinner companion. But he could have been a cardboard cutout for all the real attention she gave him.

Reece frowned at his twice-emptied plate, not sure if he was more irritated at the realization that she'd basically ignored him or at how much it bothered him. A patient man, he stubbornly bided his time. After all, he'd been doing it for six years now, give or take a marriage and a brief, mind-blowing encounter. He was good at waiting. While Mitch and Belle were in the kitchen giggling like lovebirds and getting dessert, Sierra slipped out of the dining room. He followed.

"Running away?" he asked as he sneaked up behind her in the foyer.

In a blur of motion, Sierra yelped, spun around to face him and threw her purse with astonishing strength right at his face.

Lightning fast, Reece grabbed the leather missile and lowered it to his side. He raised a brow at the woman in front of him. His irritation at being attracted to her couldn't dim his appreciation for what her panting breaths did to her luscious breasts.

Her black silk tank, so sedate and ladylike at dinner, grew tighter with every inhalation. He could just make out the lacy fabric of her bra beneath. And, his body realized with instant hardening appreciation, the outline of her nipples.

Mouth going dry at the sight, Reece craved to taste those straining peaks through the lace. Despite their hot and crazy encounter in the closet at Mitch's resort, Reece had never actually seen Sierra naked. His brain stuttered as he imagined the glorious sight. He'd explored every delicious inch of her body and devoted many hours to dreaming about how good she'd felt.

But seeing her naked? Nope. And from the irritated look on her face, those stalker shots, computer-generated abominations that they were bound to be, were the closest he was going to get.

"Is this an invitation to go with you?" he asked, reining in his fantasies and handing her the black leather bag.

"I'm sorry I threw it," she murmured. "You startled me. I guess I'm a little edgier than I thought."

Reece glanced at the door. He remembered her earlier offer to hide. "Edgy enough to run off?"

"I wasn't going anywhere," she said quickly. "I was checking my messages." Interesting that she'd instantly honed in on his suspicion. "Is this how you handle security for your clients? By sneaking up and hounding them?"

"Hounding? C'mon, sweetheart. You and I both know I might sneak under your skin from time to time—" his appreciative gaze trailed a caress over that skin, just like his fingers itched to do "—but I've never hounded you. You're just a little jumpy."

With good reason, he was about to say. But her sneer stopped him. God, if he wasn't already crazy about her, that look alone would have sent him over the edge. Pure sexual challenge, the curl of her glistening red lips made him crave a taste of the soft flesh.

"I'm only edgy when some huge, irritating guy follows me around for no reason."

"So you remember me as huge, huh?" he asked with a wicked grin, referencing aloud for the first time their little encounter at Mitch's resort. Up-against-the-wall, no-holds-barred sex that had kept him awake many a night since.

Her luscious lower lip fell, just a little, as she stared, speechless. Heat, fast and intense, flashed in her blue eyes. The look, brief though it was, assured him that nothing about their closet encounter had slipped her mind. And, thank God, the swift glance she slid to his zipper guaranteed those moans of pleasure he'd tortured himself with nightly had been the real deal.

"A huge pain in my butt, yes," she said, as if she wasn't looking at him as though she'd like to take his zipper down with her teeth.

How the hell did she do that? More to the point, why the hell did she do it? The attraction between them was right there, so obvious she had to see it. But would she acknowledge it? No. Deal with it? Hell, no.

She was driving him nuts.

Screw caution.

Furious, although he couldn't pinpoint exactly why, Reece strode forward. Two steps was all he needed to bring him close enough to feel her quickening breath against his chest. To see her pupils dilate. Whether her reaction was one of fury or the desire she denied, he didn't care. Any response other than disdain would do at this point.

All he cared about was tasting her. Proving to himself that his memories were real.

Before she could snap out whatever snippy thing was burning on the tip of her tongue, he grabbed her shoulders. Pulling her close, he grinned down into her shocked face.

"Didn't your momma ever warn you about riling a horny bull, sweetheart?"

Then he took her mouth. Under different circumstances, with a different woman, he'd have gone the gentlemanly route and coaxed the passion from her. With Sierra, he met power with power. He didn't wait for an invitation. Instead he welcomed himself into the wet heat of her mouth with a swift thrust of his tongue.

She slapped her hands onto his chest as if to push him away. But one stroke, then two, of his tongue and her hands clenched his pecs instead, fingers curling and uncurling like a kneading cat.

Her purr of pleasure sent him from turned-on to rock-hard instantly. Tongues twined, lips meshed as he gave over to the heady flash of power. Their kiss was a smooth dance, intense and sexual.

His hands slid from her shoulders, down her arms, and he entwined his fingers in hers. Needing more, he pressed her forward until her back was to the wall, trapping her between the wainscoting and his body.

Their kiss, already hot, went into overdrive. She sucked his tongue into the silky depths of her mouth, the movement mimicking a blow job of epic proportions.

Reece groaned in desperate pleasure at the image. His dick, already rock-hard, strained painfully at the teasing reminder of what it wasn't getting.

He took her hand, still linked with his, and slid it down his body. When he pressed it to his zipper, she gasped. Then her fingers clenched the rigid denim. She spread her fingers wide, moaning when they didn't cover the length of him.

"Sierra?"

They both heard Belle call from the other room at the same time. Reece had to force himself to pull back. To resist the urge to grab her and drag her to the nearest room, where he could shut and lock the door. His breath coming fast, he met Sierra's eyes.

Passion and something else blurred the blue depths. Then, with a flick of her long black lashes, it was gone. She gave his throbbing dick a soft pat, then withdrew her fingers. Her raised brow indicated she wanted loose.

Stepping away, Reece obliged.

"Sometimes huge is a good thing," he said softly as she walked back toward the kitchen.

"And sometimes," she said just as softly over her shoulder, "it just gets in the way."

3

SIERRA TUCKED a stray hair into her low ponytail and smoothed her palm over the stark white skirt of her poplin shirtdress. To keep the look from being *too* sweet, she'd paired the simple dress with red accessories and a killer pair of red leather heels. A fashionable yet unthreatening look that she hoped would put CEO Corinne Perkins and the rest of the uptight and upright Family powers-that-be at ease.

The elevator dinged her floor and she gripped her laptop case tighter as she joined the crowd pouring out. A glance at her watch assured her she was ten minutes early for the meeting. She'd intended to be twenty, but had been distracted by another photo delivery. This one had come with a note, too.

I'm Watching You.

Those three words had freaked her out. Even now, it was all she could do not to hide in the pseudo safety of the elevator.

Someone was serious about messing with her. And while she'd followed Belle's mandate and furiously pored over their client list, noting every competitor or employee she'd ever pissed off, Sierra didn't think they'd find the answer there.

Whoever was behind this was after her. Specifically. Not the company. It was too personal, too nasty to be anything else. And while she'd like to think she was woman enough to make a lasting impression on her past lovers, none of them were behind this. If they were, she reasoned, they'd know enough to make the pictures more realistic. They'd add in the mole on her hip, for instance.

As she forced herself out of the elevator, she fought back the biting grip of terror that had taken hold after the messages started arriving. The derogatory attacks on her worth, the slams on her sexuality. The ever-so-familiar insults that she hadn't heard since she'd left her aunt and uncle's home.

Anger and fear tangled together in her gut, but she ordered herself to shove them aside. Calling on all her control, she sucked in a deep breath and decided she could worry about it later. Her priority right now was nailing all the particulars of this account, and she'd be damned if she was going to let some pervert ruin it. Belle was counting on her. And more important, her own dreams were riding on it.

After that little pep talk and a few deep breaths, she greeted the HTT Publications receptionist and followed the conservative blonde into the boardroom. Belle and their favorite photographer were already there. Sierra was glad to see they were the only ones in the starkly modern room. She needed a few more minutes to shore up her composure.

"Sierra, great timing. You can tell Tristan what you think of his new look." Belle gestured with wide eyes to the man sitting at the other end of the table. "He won't believe me when I say he looks great."

Catching Belle's signal, Sierra made a show of checking out the photographer's version of conservative. The entire team had agreed that this account was important enough to toe the line, which in Tristan's case meant looking a little less over-the-top artist and a little…safer.

Taking in his transformation, Sierra wasn't sure he really understood safe. No longer in a ponytail, his pitch-black hair was short and edgy, and his slumberous midnight eyes had that just-out-of-bed-with-a-half-dozen-women look in them. He'd

even worn a suit, although the pegged black slacks and baggy
pinstriped jacket over a T-shirt might be pushing that designa-
tion just a little.

"Great look," she told him, meaning it. He was still gorgeous
and artsy, but not so out-there that he'd freak out their conservative client. She hoped. "How many gals' phone numbers did
you get on the elevator ride up here?"

His mouth quirked into a grin and he shrugged. "Just the receptionist. She thinks she'd like to try and get into fashion
modeling and wants my help with her portfolio."

Sierra and Belle exchanged looks. The wild thing was,
Tristan really thought the sweet little blonde was interested in
his camerawork. For all his sexual energy and artistic eccen-
tricities, the guy was a total innocent in many ways.

Baffling.

"Well, when the two of you are talking fashion," she said,
"be sure to keep in mind that this company prides itself on its
conservative values. So no boinking on her desk."

"Especially if the bosses are around," Belle added with a
smirk as she set up the planning and timeline boards.

"Even if they aren't," Sierra cautioned with a frown. The
three of them had been friends since high school. They all
knew how many sexual shenanigans Tristan had been caught
in. "We've busted our butts to get this account and they have
some very flimsy cancellation clauses in the contract. Even a
hint of impropriety and they'll yank this from us faster than you
can zip your pants."

"Hey," Belle admonished quietly. Her look was a mixture
of surprise and chastisement.

Sierra grimaced and jerked her shoulder. "Sorry. You know
what I mean, though."

Instead of looking offended or bothering to defend his
penchant for landing in bed with four out of five women he met,

Tristan just gave her one of his scrutinizing looks and asked, "You okay? You seem a little tense. Maybe you should get a massage when we're done here. I know a gal—she'd fit you in."

Sierra was horrified when tears filled her eyes. She blinked fast and furiously. Oh, no. There was no way she was giving in to the emotions ripping through her gut. Instead, she turned quickly to unpack her laptop so Belle wouldn't notice before she regained control.

"I'm sorry for being snappy," she said with a bright smile when she faced them again. "I'm just concerned. We're heavily invested in this job already and we're still without a long-term contract. The lack of commitment is starting to get to me."

After shooting her a worried look, Belle took the hint and changed the subject, asking Tristan, "You've confirmed your schedule is workable for their proposed dates?"

Sierra grimaced. Just another reason this account—while essential if they wanted to grab the next rung on the ladder to success—was a pain in the ass. The company was so worried about image, it wouldn't commit to any event until it had been approved by the entire board. Which meant dates and times couldn't be etched in stone. Eventfully Yours was on its third event and the first one involving the media, and the client was still waffling.

"Toby assured me my schedule is flexible," Tristan said, sitting there like an oasis of calm as Belle and Sierra fluttered around setting up their presentation, tweaking a board here, a swatch of fabric there.

Toby was Tristan's assistant and deserved a lot of credit for his success. Oh, the photographer was amazing. A great eye, incredible skill and vision had made him one of the top in California. But he tended to forget everything when he was immersed in his art. Toby kept him on track.

Much like Belle said Sierra kept her on track. Sierra knew better, of course. Sierra owed her success, and her sanity, to her best friend. Which meant she also owed her the truth.

"Ready to rock?" Belle asked quietly with a glance at her watch. One o'clock, straight up. Presentation time.

Sierra looked over and saw worry lurking in Belle's sea-green eyes. The guilt and fear crept higher in Sierra's belly. Confessions could wait. The truth would only make Belle upset.

An hour and forty minutes later, they wound up their meeting by shaking hands and, thank God, signing the contract. Corinne Perkins was a tiny white-haired woman who looked as if she would be more at home baking cookies for her grandkids than running a huge business. But she was the CEO for Family and a dynamo who demanded one hundred and twenty percent from herself and everyone else.

"Ladies," she said after Tristan had flirted his way out the door, "I'm delighted with your choice. I'll admit, I had to talk fast to get the board to agree to use a photographer with such, well, shall we say, eclectic tastes. But his work will give a modern and, I hope, urban feel to our magazine."

"Your target demographic will love his work," Belle assured the older woman. "Like the rest of our campaign, this will definitely bring in the type of advertisers and accounts you're focusing on."

Corinne smiled and stood up to hand Belle the signed contract. The stack of papers on her desk scattered and she tut-tutted as she gathered them back up. With a look of surprise, as if she hadn't noticed it before, she slid a large envelope out of the untidy pile.

Sliding her own laptop into its case, Sierra caught sight of the plain brown envelope and purple mailing label. Her stomach took a dive.

What the hell? It couldn't be.

Corinne slid an unmanicured nail under the flap. Sierra wanted to lunge across the desk and grab the envelope. But she couldn't. She was frozen in her chair, her brain going a million miles a second, her body held in terrified stasis.

Corinne withdrew a small piece of paper out of the envelope. She gasped and threw it on the desk.

Sierra closed her eyes, too horrified to look.

"No," Belle breathed. Eyes still closed, Sierra felt rather than saw her partner drop to the chair next to her.

The silence in the room was heavy.

"Care to explain this?" Corinne finally snapped.

Unable to continue hiding, Sierra forced herself to look.

Corinne was pointing a shaking finger at the piece of five-by-seven ugliness. Sierra winced. Obviously pervy boy had found a Photoshop for morons guide, because this picture looked real. Sierra, three guys and a whole slew of sex toys. Sierra was clueless as to what they even were. Apparently the men had no such problem, since they were using most of them on each other.

In danger of losing her lunch, she pressed her hand to her stomach. In bold white text across the black-and-white image were the words *Sluts Are Bad For Business*.

"I…" She couldn't even speak. The words just stuck in her throat, pitiful and apologetic. A familiar feeling of being judged and found guilty washed over her.

"Corinne, I'm horrified you've been brought into this," Belle said, talking fast, but with that girl-to-girl confidant tone that suggested she was sharing secrets. She went on to describe the evolution of the stalker pictures, pointing out the few clues that would assure their very uptight client that this was a digitally enhanced image. She ended with, "We've involved the police, and I assure you the matter is being dealt with."

Through it all, Sierra just stared at the photo and tried to breathe. Everything they'd worked for. Everything she'd wanted since she'd escaped to boarding school—security, acceptance, independence—all seemed to be disintegrating under the weight of that picture.

"Ladies, I…" The CEO hesitated, then tapped her finger on their hard-won contract. "I believe you. I honestly do. But this isn't the kind of thing that Family Publications can find itself connected to."

Corinne sighed, then flipped the picture over. She grimaced, as if not liking what she was about to say.

"I hate to do it, but I might need to rethink things," she said, flattening her hand over the contract. "While you girls have the best outline of events, programs and entertainment for our board and sponsors, this kind of thing can't be tolerated. Family, as you know, would be horrified to find itself associated with anything of this nature."

"There's no way they could be," Sierra said breathlessly. Geez, unless the creep got the board members' faces and pasted them into the next orgy shot, how could this affect them? She was the one the guy was after. Her past was coming back to haunt her. She was sure of it. That realization froze the rest of her argument in her throat. Her past? Was it possible that her uncle had decided to stop his favorite game of blackmail and turn his dirty hand to photo stalking? No. There was no payoff here that he cared about. It was just the work of some sick pervert.

How pathetic that the idea was a reassurance.

"They don't even have to know," Belle interrupted. "The problem is being investigated and will be resolved any day now."

Sierra had to force her lips together. Who knew Belle could lie to someone's face like that?

"We've not only involved the police, but we've hired a

private security firm. We'll be happy to bring them to the events if it would reassure you."

Another ten minutes of building on that lie and Belle had convinced the woman to leave their contract alone.

Sierra kept her face neutral until Corinne left the boardroom.

"I can't believe you bullshitted her like that," she hissed. "How long do you think it'll take before she notices we don't have security?"

"We do." Belle stood and ripped her board from the wall. "Reece can handle the security."

Ignoring that just the mention of his name turned her on, Sierra sneered. Reece, help her? She started to laugh, then stopped. Maybe that wasn't a bad idea. Of course, he wouldn't do it for her, but he would for Belle. He had the credentials. Mr. Security could pretend perfectly.

"Will he agree? Can you call him and ask?" This was doable, she told herself. If they handled it right, she wouldn't even have to see the cowboy. Belle could ask him, maybe bring him around to meet Corinne and do the whole fake security-assurance thing. All Sierra had to do was smile and keep her mouth shut.

Impossible. She was ruining everything. Now Belle was having to lie for her. And worse, they would have to bring Reece into the whole humiliating mess.

"I should just step aside. I can do the behind-the-scenes work for a while." Her offer held a hint of desperation. "Work from home, keep a low profile."

"Don't let this guy run you off," Belle said. "Reece will help. That's all we need. He's already offered. He told Mitch and I that he'd step in at any time. You just have to ask him." Sierra opened her mouth to protest, but Belle shook her head before she could say anything. "No. You have to do the asking. It's only fair."

"I think it'd come much better from you," Sierra protested.

After all, the last time she'd talked to him, she'd patted his dick and walked away.

"Look," Belle said as she shoved the boards into her portfolio case, "we need this account. We've invested too much in the job already. I don't want you to step aside, so we need security. *You* need security. He's already agreed. All you have to do is talk to him."

Sierra sighed at the fond memory of a much less ballsy Belle. The one who'd easily backed off from confrontation and let people live—and screw up—their lives in peace.

Except this wasn't just Sierra's life being screwed up. Now it was her—their—business. The one Belle had brought her into. Belle saw them as equals, and it would be because of Sierra if they failed.

"I'll talk to him," she agreed reluctantly.

"Now."

"I have—"

"No excuses. Go see him before he leaves town. He's working out of Mitch's downtown office."

Sierra's jaw ached as she struggled to hold back an ugly retort. Instead, she dug into her purse for a piece of peppermint candy and, with short, jerky movements, unwrapped it and shoved it into her mouth. Maybe the sugar would sweeten her mood. God knew, she'd need it if she was going to go asking favors of Reece Carter.

REECE HAD TO hand it to the twists of fate. Just when he'd written off any shot with Sierra, she walked through his door asking for a favor. Sure, she looked as if she'd rather be having a root canal and was as edgy as if she'd just killed someone. But she was here. Life was never boring, that was for sure.

"Look, I just need you to come by the client's office and

pretend to be Eventfully Yours' security." He noticed she wasn't calling it *her* security. That would be admitting too much. "Just fake it so we don't lose this job."

Reece shook his head. "Sweetheart, I already offered to do the job. But the deal is, if I'm in, I'm all the way in."

He let his words lie there between them, enjoying the image. Enjoying even more Sierra's reaction to it. She turned pale, then blushed. As the rose faded from her cheeks, she just glared at him.

"If you want me, it's for real. Not some fake bullshit to con your client. You'd need to listen to me, do what I say when it comes to protecting you from this creep."

The look on her face, pure fury, told him that she didn't want him at all. He read her body signals, the way her legs tensed, her fingers curling around the handle of her briefcase. She wanted to storm out, probably flipping him off on her way. But she stayed seated.

This must be one hell of an account on the line.

"You're no better than the pervy jerk with the computer program," she accused in a tone that barely disguised her underlying frustration. "It's all about the sex for you guys. He's trying to humiliate me with sex. You're just out to get a piece of ass."

It took every ounce of Reece's training to keep his expression blank. Anger clawed at his gut, aching to be released in a slew of cutting words.

His army major's number one dictum rang in his head. *It's nothing personal.* He used the phrase to get himself under control.

"Want to let me see the pictures?" he said, shoving aside his fury with an effort. Ripping into her was pointless. She was already being terrorized. Besides, he'd get his way. They both knew it, so there was no point in hammering it home and making her feel any worse.

She stared at him in silence for ten seconds. Then twenty.

At thirty, she seemed to crumble. Women's tears didn't scare him, but the stoic fear on Sierra's dry-eyed face ripped at his gut. He wanted nothing more than to pull her into his arms and promise to keep her safe, to hide her away until he'd found and dealt with the asshole causing her such misery.

But then she lifted her chin and pulled a thick envelope from her case. It wasn't until she stood and walked over to hand him the package that he realized she'd kicked off her shoes. She was tiny without them, barely reaching his shoulder. The image only added to his protective urges.

Until she opened her mouth.

"Did you want privacy to look at them?" she murmured with a shaky smirk as she held them out.

"There's nothing I'd do in private that I wouldn't rather do with you in the room, sweetheart," he shot back as he opened the package. His temper lurked in the words, lingering irritation that she'd accuse him of being all about sex. Sure, he wanted her. But this was business. He was a big boy and knew the difference.

He didn't shift from where he sat, one hip leaning on the desk, but he did come to attention as he flipped through the photos. With each one, his frown deepened. His impression from both Belle and Mitch was that this was a simple harassment situation. Some guy Sierra had blown off trying to get her attention, maybe.

Now he thought different. This was ugly. The escalating obsession, the tightening focus. The sexual threat.

The son of a bitch behind this was one sick mother. And he was obsessed with Sierra. Reece's gut burned. He blinked twice to clear the red haze of fury from his gaze.

No point in scaring Sierra any more than she already was. But the reality was, the little brunette was in serious shit here.

"Sweetheart, I'm going to be your new best friend," he told her with an easy smile as he tucked the pictures back in their protective brown covering and tossed them onto the desk behind him.

"I'm covered there, thanks so much," she shot back, her usual sass returning along with the color in her cheeks. "How about you just lurk in the background and discourage perverts, hmm?"

Reece smirked, waiting.

Sierra gave a sigh and rolled her eyes. "Fine, I'm sorry I called you a pervy jerk out to get in my pants, okay? I realize you're many steps above the creep that's pulling this stunt."

Enjoying himself, Reece just continued to stare.

Sierra's lips quirked but she didn't say anything. Just crossed her arms, which was a shame since they covered her breasts, and leaned back in the chair.

Power play? Reece's smirk turned into a full-fledged grin. No wonder he couldn't get Sierra out of his head. He loved nothing more than a challenge. At least, until he'd conquered it.

With that in mind, he let his gaze turn slumberous. All it took was the thought of her lips under his. He recalled their encounter in Mitch's hall a few days back. The delicious taste of her, the feel of her breath as it warmed his skin. He mentally traced those lips with his gaze, watching their glossy fullness press together in irritation.

The phone at his hip rang, but Reece didn't take his eyes from Sierra's. Her gaze was molten now, a deep blue filled with sexual heat and awareness. Her lashes fluttered, as if she wanted to pull away but couldn't bring herself to.

"Mr. Carter?"

He didn't release Sierra's gaze to look at the woman in the doorway, but did answer her. "Yeah?"

"Mr. Driscol on line one. He'd like to discuss expanding his offer." Her voice hesitated as she apparently picked up on the tension in the room, then she cleared her throat and continued, "He said the timing is crucial and he needs an answer ASAP."

Driscol was a client who liked Reece's way of doing security. He liked it so much he wanted Reece to move RC

Security out here to Southern California to be on a permanent retainer.

No doing, though. Reece had already told the guy twice. Nothing could entice him to move his base here to L.A. Crowds, crime and crazies. None of which appealed more than the wide open spaces of his home in Kentucky. His family was there, his grandma and his dad. Travel was all well and good, but he needed to know he could drop in for Sunday dinner anytime he wanted. After all, that sense of family was his touchstone, his reminder of everything that mattered to him.

Mitch had been begging him to relocate here, too. But if he wasn't going to do it for a cousin he loved, he sure wasn't about to move for a job he didn't need.

"I'll call him back."

"But…"

"I'll call him back," Reece repeated.

"Yes, sir," she murmured as she left, closing the door.

"Shall we discuss terms?" Reece asked, refocusing his attention on Sierra.

"Don't you have a contract for that?" she asked, her tone deliberately breezy. She must have used the interruption to think. And her conclusion was to ignore the heated sexual tension sparking between them.

He'd have to see how quickly he could change that.

"I realize you're exactly the kind of client I generally turn away," he pointed out.

"You mean the kind that doesn't worship you?"

Reece laughed. "A little worship wouldn't hurt. But no, I mean the kind that doesn't listen. If I'm going to protect you, you have to agree that I'm in charge. I can't do my job unless you're willing to give me your complete cooperation."

"You never struck me as the have-to-be-on-top kind of guy, cowboy."

Reece gave her a slow grin and waited. It didn't take more than two seconds for her to realize that she knew firsthand that he was all about equal opportunities when it came to sexual positions.

"You'll do exactly as I say?" was all he said, though.

Her jaw tensed in a sharp line and he watched her delicate fingers tighten into fists. She stared at him, then dropped her gaze to the package of pictures on the desk. Her brow furrowed and a tiny shudder shook her shoulders. Then, as if to shrug it off, she lifted one shoulder and tilted her head toward him.

"I'll do exactly what you say," she agreed. Reece let the pleasure of those words wash over him. "But…"

"Of course there's a but."

"But," she continued, sliding her feet back into those killer heels and standing, "only as it applies to this picture perv, Family and the necessary protection required so Eventfully Yours doesn't lose the account."

Once she was in her high heels again, her game face firmly in place, all of the vulnerability that had scared Reece was gone. Sierra was back in control.

Just the way he liked her.

"Works for me," he agreed, stepping forward and holding out his hand.

She shook her head. Apparently she had other caveats. "This account is crucial. My work, my focus right now has to be one hundred percent."

He waited.

She frowned, and for the first time since he'd met her, she looked as if she was trying to find an inoffensive way to word her request.

Then she shrugged and rolled her eyes. "I can't waste time deflecting your attempts at sexual games. I need to work. I don't have time to worry about you hitting on me."

He couldn't help it. He laughed.

Sierra hissed.

"Sweetheart, I won't have to hit. I promise." He reached across her to put his hand on the door handle. "A week, maybe less, and you'll be the one hitting."

"You think pretty damned highly of yourself," she said with a strained laugh.

"We're about to do the one thing you've been avoiding since we first met six years ago." He paused, watching her eyes turn smoky blue.

He could see exactly what was going through her pretty head and grinned down at her in appreciation. She was thinking sex, pure and simple. Or not so simple, in their case. He loved that about her. Not only was she a deeply sensual being, but she didn't try to hide it. There was nothing coy or demure about Sierra Donovan. She was all woman and embraced her sexuality with both hands. Even if she didn't want to share it with him.

That was okay. She hadn't wanted to share before, either. That hadn't stopped them from doing it against a wall. The sexual pull between them was more intense than anything he'd ever felt. He had complete faith it would overwhelm her again.

Eventually. He just had to push the right buttons.

"What's that?" she finally asked in a husky tone.

"We're going to spend a whole lot of time together, sweetheart. I promise, time is all I need to chip away at that mile-high wall of resistance you like to hide behind."

He turned the handle and pulled the door open.

She stared for a second longer, then stepped toward the door, her breast brushing his forearm as she turned away and said, "You wouldn't like what's on the other side."

"Time in bed, you mean."

Reece sneered at the innuendo that all he wanted from Sierra was sex. Damn, it was one thing to get that from her. She had no reason to trust him. Yet. And he'd noticed she had a mile-deep cynicism that lent itself to thinking the worst of men. But his own cousin?

Mitch should realize there was more to Reece's interest than just sex. Yeah, maybe it'd been lust at first sight when he'd seen Sierra six years ago. When he'd hit on her, then spent his entire leave trying to convince her that one date with him wouldn't betray her friend, who'd just left his cousin at the altar. But lust alone would have burned out after six years apart. Not been kept alive all those nights when he'd bunked down in the desert.

It wouldn't have been secretly nurtured during his ill-fated marriage.

Even obsessive lust would have been slaked a couple months ago when she'd kissed him and he'd lost all control. He'd like to claim it was shock that had sent his libido into overdrive and his finesse out the window. But that'd be a lie and he never lied. At least, not to himself.

Nope, it'd been idiot lust that had him taking her up against the wall like a horny teenager chasing his first glimpse of heaven.

Just sex? Hell, no. This was bigger than just wanting to get laid.

But he realized how it would sound if he tried to defend himself. Lovesick and pitiful. Wincing, he sucked down another swallow of beer. Nope. Innuendo was better.

"Not saying I don't want to get her in my bed," he admitted as Mitch slid two overflowing plates onto the small kitchen table and sat opposite him. "But I hardly need to resort to grade-school games to get her there. I'm asking for the case."

Mitch rolled his eyes before he bit into his own sandwich. Then, after a swig of beer, he shrugged. "Sierra doesn't really date. I mean, sure, she'll do dinner or the theater with a guy here or there. But in the month Belle and I have been living together, I've never met a guy Sierra's been out with."

"Maybe she just keeps them to herself?"

"She doesn't keep anything from Belle."

"And Belle doesn't keep anything from you?" Reece was the one smirking this time. Women, in his experience, weren't known for their forthcoming honesty or willingness to share. Even if he did think Belle was the sweetest thing since melted chocolate, she was still female.

"Belle's not Shawna," Mitch said tonelessly.

Reece grimaced. Whether at the mention of his ex-wife or at the fact that he'd just pissed off his cousin, he wasn't sure. Didn't matter.

"Look, I'm not saying Belle hides things from you," Reece said, biting into his sandwich. He chewed and swallowed before clarifying. "I'm just wondering if she'd waste your lovey-dovey couple time talking about her business partner's love life."

"Hey, she told me Sierra did you up against a wall," Mitch said with a snicker as he polished off his lunch.

Nonplussed, Reece dropped his sandwich and stared. God, did women really share everything? He blamed the heat warming his cheeks on the beer and forced himself not to take the bait and ask for details. He would ask Sierra himself if she'd liked it, thank you. No way was he fishing for that info via his smirking cousin.

"Whoever is stalking her has a personal vendetta and the pictures are definitely a sexual message."

Changing the subject before Mitch could rib him, Reece thought of the file in his briefcase. He'd copied all the photos and threatening messages. He forced himself to think unemotionally. "If you're right and the only sex she's been talking about is with me, then we need to look at a different motive," he decided.

Not that he really believed a woman as hot as Sierra was going without the last two months. But the distance created in most of the photo montages hinted at worship from afar, not pained rejection.

"So you don't think there's a sexual motive?" Mitch asked as he carried their empty plates over to the sink.

"I think sex is integral to the motive," Reece mused, "but I don't think it's necessarily the reason behind it. There's also an element of revenge going on here."

He stared at the wall, mulling over the possibilities. And coming up blank.

"I'm not ruling anything out," he decided, his fingers itching to sketch out the details on paper. He always thought more clearly when he charted the ideas, all the possibilities. Spying a notepad and pen by the phone, he got up to grab it, then straddled the chair again. Pushing the Stetson off his forehead, he considered, then wrote.

Sex. Money. Morals. Clients. Pictures. Fake. Altered.

"Figure it out?" Mitch asked twenty minutes later.

As if coming out of a fog, Reece shrugged off the contemplative trance and glanced at his cousin.

"Nope. Not even close." He looked at the page again and pulled a face. He'd have to dig deeper. Check into her past. Reece grimaced. Wouldn't she love that? "I have a start, though. That's good enough for now."

Mitch laughed, a mocking bark of humor. "For now? You realize those women expect you to have this solved before their event tomorrow, right?"

Reece shrugged. Somehow, he always failed to meet women's expectations. Especially the ones that mattered. "Nothing to be done," he muttered. "Sierra is already used to me not doing what she expects."

"It doesn't sound like you'll wind this up fast, then?"

"It'll take as long as it takes. The first priority is keeping Sierra safe. Second is keeping the damage to their business as minimal as possible."

Neither man had to say that the priority list was just between the two of them. The women would pitch a fit, Reece was sure, to hear their business wasn't number one.

"So you'll be sticking around for a while?"

"As long as it takes," he repeated.

Fortunately for Reece, his business was such that he could handle the bulk of it from anywhere. Thanks to his laptop and cell phone, he could hole up on his ranch for twenty out of thirty-one days each month if he wanted.

And he usually wanted. Years of army life had left him with a need for open spaces and minimal contact with people for long stretches of time. He was already getting itchy here in L.A. with its crowds of bodies and buildings.

RC Security was, for the most part, simple investigations. He had a team of six guys who handled security, protection and a lot of the legwork for him. The bulk of his job was similar to what he'd done for Mitch's resort. Set up a security system, hire and train the personnel, spot-check and reevaluate regularly.

"Since you're here for a while anyway, are you going to consider Driscol's offer?" Mitch asked, his words overly casual.

"I just don't see myself as an urban cowboy, if you know what I mean. The offer is intriguing, though. Handling security on such a large and complex level would be a challenge."

"But?"

Reece tapped his pen on the paper as he weighed the options. He loved Mitch like a brother, but that wasn't a good enough reason to change his life.

"But," he finally said, "he's adamant that his security chief headquarter here in California. I'd take the job in a heartbeat if it wasn't for that sticking point."

Mitch pulled a face and gazed over Reece's shoulder at the view out the window. Gathering his thoughts, Reece knew.

"Ya know, there's a lot to keep you here. Great job offer, family—" he shot Reece a wicked smile "—a smart woman you're totally hot for."

"I've got a great job already," Reece shot back. "Most of the family is in Kentucky. Dad's lonely with Mom gone. It'd be cruel to leave him, and he's not about to move to the land of the flakes and nuts. I'm needed at home. Besides, no woman is worth moving for." A little voice in the back of his head argued that Sierra could be. But he'd learned the hard way that sacrificing for a woman was the first step toward a long, painful fall to misery.

"Sierra isn't Shawna, either." Mitch didn't say it, but he obviously thought Reece was using the wrong yardstick to measure women.

"Nope, she's not," Reece agreed in a slow, easy drawl that hid his irritation at the silent admonishment. "She's worse. She's everything Shawna wished she could be. Confident, successful and independent."

"Those aren't bad things."

Not bad? Shawna's determination to be all those things had turned her into a nagging shrew and almost bankrupted Reece. Determined to get even the knock-off version of all she wanted, she'd racked up a huge credit card debt, selling off his possessions to fuel her shopping binges and ripping his life to shreds in the process. Sierra, though, was already the real thing. He shuddered just thinking of the damage she could do.

"They are for me," Reece decided.

CLIPBOARD IN HAND, Sierra scanned the reserved area of the park.

Pristine white tents tied back with bright blue ribbon and the company's logo flags? Check.

Catering arrived and setting up? Check.

Flowers, party favors and promotional materials delivered and displayed? She noted her two assistants arranging vases of daisies and sunflowers on the various linen-covered picnic tables, each one complete with a whirligig and logo flag. No promo materials out yet, so she left that one unchecked.

Gazebo straight out of a clichéd small-town movie set, complete with three-piece band? Check.

No perverts in sight? Check.

Family had suggested renting a hotel meeting room, but she'd convinced them this was a smarter venue. Yes, there was more that could go wrong by using a public location, and an outdoor one at that. But the message the wide expanse of green grass, lush trees and bright blue sky gave was clear. Wholesome, natural and fun.

Throw in that gazebo, apple pie and a few freckle-faced kids and it was the golden ticket to good, old-fashioned values. The kind that would bring in millions in advertising dollars, she hoped.

"How's it coming together?" Belle asked as she carefully made her way across the soft grass, having to pull a spiked heel out of the lawn with each step.

"You should have worn wedges," Sierra noted with a half grin.

"I have a pair on the way," Belle returned, angling one foot to the side to note the damage to her sweet white sandals. "Along with a freezer unit for the caterers. I know the weatherman said it'd only hit the seventies, but I don't want to risk sweaty guests."

Sierra flipped a couple pages to scan the catering list. "What are you adding?" she asked, pencil poised.

"Lemonade gelato. Light, cool, just a little exotic." Belle waved away a lone bug, squinting across the lawn as if looking for its friends. "Should we bring in fans, too? They might shoo the bugs away. Better safe with two stones."

"Better safe than sorry, and it's two birds you're killing with those stones," Sierra corrected absently. She looked over the tableau herself. "Upscale outdoor entertainment. Ritzy, yet still family-friendly. Since they don't mind kids with their pâté, I think they can handle a few bugs."

Belle snickered, then a weird, freaked-out look crossed her face. Sierra immediately tucked her clipboard under her arm and asked, "What's wrong?"

"Mitch mentioned kids last night."

"As in he has a few tied up in a closet?"

Belle wrinkled her nose. "No. Just…you know, painting a picture of our future. And it included babies."

"But I thought you both agreed that you wanted kids." A baby. Sierra's heart squeezed tight at the idea of a baby. Someone to love her, unconditionally. Someone she could love without restrictions. That the baby she imagined had Reece's midnight-blue eyes was only coincidence. It didn't mean a damned thing.

"We did discuss it," Belle said with a hint of panic, "but that was hypothetical. Mitch suggesting names made it seem real."

"You'll be a great mom," Sierra told her.

"I don't know anything about kids," Belle said quietly, focusing on one of the tables. Sierra glanced over and noted it was the one with lollipop centerpieces and toys instead of party favors. "I don't know if I understand them."

"You understand love. That'll make you an excellent mom." Putting her hand on Belle's arm, she gave it a squeeze.

"Yeah?" Belle blinked fast to keep the tears from messing up her makeup. Then, in her usual perky way, she shrugged aside the heavy emotions and gave Sierra a teasing wink. "And they'll have the perfect godmother, huh?"

Sierra's heart stuttered again. Hey, if she couldn't have her own, she'd be the best godmother in the world.

Needing to move past the aching need, she changed the subject. She and Belle went over their pre-event checklist and compared tasks to make sure they were on track. Ten minutes later, assured everything was perfect, they met with Corinne and her staff, all dressed in their Sunday best.

As they went over the plans, a car door slammed, making Belle jump. Not Sierra. The only things that made her nervous these days were postal workers and cameras.

Then she saw the man walking across the lawn. Her pulse sped up. Her mouth went dry. He was pure masculine beauty, his cowboy hat shading his eyes and a pair of strappy wedge-heeled sandals dangling from his finger.

"Damn," she breathed.

Belle followed her gaze. "You knew he'd be here."

Of course she'd known. Hell, she'd arranged it in order to appease Corinne. So getting all schoolgirl-crushing-on-the-hottie giddy was ridiculous. And if she told herself that often enough, she should start believing it, right?

"Play nice," Belle warned. "We're on the job."

Stopping just short of sticking her tongue out at Belle, she forced her social smile in place. Ignoring the flickering desire taking hold in her stomach, Sierra pulled out her checklist again and took adolescent pleasure in drawing a line through her checkmark next to the no-perverts notation.

No problem. She'd make herself think of him the same way she did chilled shrimp. Something deliciously tempting, but something that caused a hideous allergic reaction in her body. Only here to make a huge impression on the client, but personally off-limits unless she wanted to deal with the resulting pain.

And life dished out enough of that. A smart gal had to stick to her no-pain policy. And Sierra was smart. Reece Carter wasn't going to get to her. Not today, not again.

With that little pep talk in mind, she double-checked her emotional walls. Yup, she was thoroughly protected. Then she made sure her tidy white cotton blouse was buttoned to hide cleavage and tucked neatly into her slim-but-not-body-hugging pencil skirt and forced herself not to wipe away her lipstick.

"Reece, you're just in time to meet our clients and give them some assurances that security is in good hands," she said in lieu of a greeting.

The glance he gave her said he knew she was trying to set solid boundaries and he'd take pleasure in tearing them down, one suggestive look at a time. But he didn't say anything. Instead he handed Belle her shoes, then gave her a kiss on the cheek and a charming smile.

"Not quite a glass slipper, but I assume these move me closer to prince status?" he teased.

"Well, they'll definitely keep me out of the squash," Belle mangled with a grin as she bent down to change into the lawn-friendly shoes.

Reece frowned at the top of her platinum head, then gave Sierra a baffled look and a shrug. She held back a smile.

"Pumpkins are squash," she deciphered quietly.

She had to give him credit. It only took a couple seconds for the fog of confusion to clear in his blue eyes. She told herself there was nothing sexy about the way they crinkled at the corners when he grinned, or the indulgent look of appreciation he shot her best friend.

Nope. And the fact that her mouth went dry at the sight and her heart beat a smidge faster didn't mean a damned thing.

"Since you're already in the princess rescue mode," she said, her words a little sharper than she'd intended, "maybe we could get to work."

"Don't be jealous, sweetheart. For you, I'll personally deliver anything you need. Shoes, clothes…satisfaction." His voice dropped to almost a whisper at the last word, keeping it just between the two of them. His gaze, hot and admiring, swept over Sierra, from the top of her hair to the tips of her toes. Like an electrical current, a zing of energy tingled everywhere his eyes rested.

"How about you deliver on your promise," she told him breathlessly. "You know the one? That you'd do a job?"

"That's what I'm here for," he assured her as if his gaze hadn't just promised untold sexual pleasure. He shot a long, intense look around the park and shook his head. "Not exactly the kind of place you'd expect to find a perverted cameraman, but I'll do my best."

"Speaking of men with cameras," Belle paraphrased, "Tristan's here, Sierra. Do you want me to do the run-through with him?"

Sierra noted Tristan and his assistant trudging through the trees. As always, the sight of Toby nagged at Sierra. He had one of those faces that made people think they'd met before. Both men were loaded down with camera equipment and looking a little shell-shocked at the wholesome scene before them.

Hmm, tough choice. Stick with the sexiest devil she knew, or prove that challenging glint in his eyes right and run off at the first opportunity. Her spine straightened with a stubborn snap. Hell, no. She wasn't running.

She met Reece's gaze, saw the sexual curiosity that always lurked in those blue depths when he looked at her. The heat of it tempted her like crazy. He shifted his body, just a smidge, and the scent of his cologne filled her senses. His body heat wrapped around her like a sensuous blanket of temptation. Calling out an invitation that her mind wanted to deny but her body was already accepting. Images of his mouth taking hers, the power of his kisses and the passion they ignited flashed in her mind.

Against her will, her nipples peaked under the heavy cotton of her blouse. She wanted to feel his lips, his teeth and tongue on the aching flesh. She wanted to see how wild he could get if they really had sex.

Not the quick and meaningless up-against-the-wall kind of sex they'd had once. But the stripped bare, eyes wide open and lights-on kind. Somehow, she knew he'd rock her world like no one ever had before. Usually she figured an orgasm was an orgasm. But with Reece? Sex with him was the stuff of legends. Her body tingled at the memory of his rigid length filling her, driving home harder and harder.

Wet, intense, wild.

God, he was incredible.

"I'll take Tristan," she decided abruptly. Without waiting to see their reaction, she turned and stomped across the lawn toward the photographer. Mocking laughter followed. It was only the sight of Corinne, waving regally, that kept her from flipping Reece the bird over her shoulder.

REECE WATCHED SIERRA storm off, not bothering to keep the grin off his face. Was there anything more satisfying than getting that kind of a reaction from a woman?

Of course there was, he corrected himself. But she wasn't stripping naked and letting him worship her with his tongue, so he'd have to settle for her fury instead.

"Guess that leaves the introductions to me," Belle said, her green eyes dancing with humor.

"You're awfully easy with this whole stalker security thing," Reece commented as he fell in beside her to walk across the lawn.

"I'm not taking the stalker situation lightly at all," she stated. "But I know you'll take care of things, so needless worrying and crying over spilled chickens is pointless."

It took him a second, then he got it. Spilled milk, chickens before they hatched. No point worrying about something that hadn't happened.

He grinned. Hey, he was getting better at deciphering his cousin-to-be's strange mind. Kudos to him.

As they approached the tent, Belle gave him a sidelong glance. "Besides, Mitch and I have a bet going on who's going to win."

There went his kudos.

Before he could ask the odds or clarify the parameters of the bet, they'd reached the mass of bodies huddled in the shade. The CEO whom he'd met the previous week when Belle briefed her on the new security measures separated herself from the pack.

"Belle, lovely arrangement. I'm so glad we took your advice on this event." Her deep, husky voice was more suited to a blues club than a G-rated magazine.

Reece flipped through his mental files on the Family connections. Moral values, middle-of-the-road politics, high-end advertisers. The corporation touted family values. He noted the big hats and below-the-knee skirts on the women and pale suits on the men. Definitely a group that would squirm in horror if they saw nasty sex pictures of their event coordinator.

"Mr. Carter, it's wonderful to see you again," the woman continued. "I'm sure you'll do a fine job handling security. We appreciate your diligence and focus. Although a more detailed report of your plans would be appreciated for the next event. I'm sure the ladies can fill you in on our requirements."

Like an overzealous bulldozer wrapped in floral chintz, she continued to micromanage at the speed of light. She grilled Belle on the event schedule, a schedule, he noted as he glanced at the blonde's clipboard, that she'd already approved.

It wasn't until she'd reprised every detail of the event with them—apparently she felt Reece needed to know the menu in order to provide security for Sierra—that she took a breath and smiled. Kind of like a large shark wearing a tacky beaded necklace.

"I'll let you get to it, then," she said, patting Belle on the arm. Reece earned a tight-lipped nod, but no body contact. He wasn't sure if it was because he was male, or considered hired help.

"By the way, I haven't received any more of those…nasty pictures," she said in a low tone, her eyes darting left and right as if someone might jump in and interrupt their conversation. "I search the mail personally every day. Just in case another one shows up, of course. I'd hate to have anyone else subjected to such a sight. I've never been so shocked in my life."

"You won't have to worry, ma'am," Reece assured her. "The situation is under control and your company won't be bothered again."

Corinne sniffed but seemed reluctantly satisfied.

Belle shot him a look of surprise at the bold promise. He didn't figure this was the time or place to explain that he'd made a deal with the guy in the mailroom to make sure no envelopes matching the stalker's style made it to the client's desk.

"And speaking of pictures, please do remind your photographer to be careful with his shots," Corinne warned. "I've heard his upcoming show is quite…well, risqué. I don't want to see anything of that nature in our proofs."

With that last admonishment and a wave of her fingers, she left, trailing the smell of rose water and hairspray.

"Show?" Reece asked quietly as he turned to see Belle release a slow, silent sigh.

Belle raised one finger, her lips barely moving. He frowned. Was she muttering silently under her breath? He saw her reach ten, then keep going.

"What show?" he repeated.

Belle pressed her lips together, glared at him, then looked around and waved a hand before starting over at one.

He followed her gesture. His gut tensed, fury and suspicion filling his belly at the sight of Sierra laughing, her hand on the arm of some guy. Reece's gaze narrowed. Six foot, built like a runner, black hair and eyes, an air of sexual energy and a GQ-meets-artist persona.

"Who the hell is that?" he asked.

"Tristan's our photographer. His work is being featured in an erotic art exhibit this weekend."

Reece watched the guy put his arm around Sierra and waited. But she didn't shrug it off. Instead she grinned up at the guy like a hypnotized groupie.

Photographer, huh? Erotic art? Reece tipped his Stetson back and stared across the lawn.

Metro boy had just moved to the top of the suspect list.

5

THREE HOURS LATER, Sierra stormed into her office. She threw her purse at the corner chair with enough force that it bounced off the soft cushion and ricocheted against the rich wood of the étagère.

"Just who the hell do you think you are?" she demanded as she spun around, almost stuttering in her fury. "How dare you try and humiliate me and embarrass one of my associates. If that wasn't bad enough, you did it in front of our clients? What the hell were you thinking?"

Through the hazy red spots dancing in her vision, she glared at Reece as he sauntered through the door. One look at her face and he turned, quietly closed the door behind him, then leaned against it. Arms crossed, that stupid hat shading his eyes and one ankle cocked over the other, he looked as if he were waiting for a damned stagecoach.

Sierra wanted to beat him upside the head with his own hat, then toss him out the window and hope a bus would run his ass over.

"I asked you a question." She ground the words out, then slammed her fists on her hips and waited. There was no way his cutesy drawl and aw-shucks grin were going to save his sorry butt this time. No way at all.

"Was that a question?" he asked, his tone barely interested. "I thought it was more along the lines of the opening salvo to a temper tantrum."

Sierra's mouth worked, but no words came out.

"After all, you already know quite well who I am." His mouth quirked a little at the corner, as if he knew her brain had just offered a whole slew of suggestions of just exactly what he was, too. "And before you toss out the next clichéd attack, you know damned well what I thought I was doing, too."

His calm tone, as well as his refusal to accept that he'd been a complete and total ass, astonished Sierra. Enough so that she was able to sublimate her anger. Not eliminate it. She was too furious to just shut it away. But she was able to think around it now. To use it.

And more importantly, to make damned sure he didn't use it against her. She knew from experience—pleasurable, to be sure—that losing her temper around Reece gave him the advantage. And he usually took it.

Not this time. Any advantage would be hers. Forcing herself to breathe normally, she dropped her hands from her hips and tilted her head as if to study him while she mentally solidified her plan of attack.

"You thought you'd make a total ass out of yourself while mocking my business?" she mused, tapping one finger on her chin as she raised a brow. "Or, let's see, maybe you were overcome by the uptight, conservative atmosphere and couldn't resist trying to bring it down to street level?"

"You say that as if I started a brawl in the middle of your church social." He gave her a long look that clearly implied he thought she was overreacting. It also said he didn't mind the results. Sierra didn't have to glance down to know her chest was flushed, her nipples probably stiff.

"You might as well have," Sierra pointed out, trying to distract him, if not herself. "You verbally assaulted one of my employees in full hearing of the CEO and board of the clients we were trying to pacify."

"Verbal assault?" His laugh was short and hard. That and the dark look in his eyes actually scared Sierra a little. It also turned her on. Her breath quickened a little, the emotions flying out of control and coalescing into an edgy desire.

She couldn't let him win.

"Pacify," she repeated as if he hadn't interrupted. The words tripped over themselves as she tried to bury her desire in anger. "Because they are not only an important, lucrative account, but are key to a whole new level of business that Belle and I have busted our asses to get."

"I didn't—"

"You almost ruined it," she interrupted, "with your macho attack on my photographer. When you hauled him off for public interrogation, you made him and us look like idiots. The last thing I need right now is…is…"

At that point, she lost it.

Striding forward, she emphasized each of her words by poking her index finger into his rock-hard chest.

"Any…" Poke.

"Stupid…" Poke.

"Male…" Poke.

"Sexual…" Poke.

"Posturing." Three pokes for emphasis.

The last finger jab might have been too much. Reece grabbed her hand, wrapping his own much larger, much stronger one around hers in a firm, yet still gentle grip.

"That wasn't posturing, sweetheart. That was me doing the job I agreed to do."

"You were supposed to appease our client," she hissed.

"I was supposed to provide protection while finding out who is photographically stalking you."

"Neither of which you were doing there while you played my-dick-is-bigger-than-yours with Tristan."

She knew damned well the clients had noted as much, since many of them had gathered together murmuring and sending morbidly curious looks at the two men. That nobody had complained was only a matter of luck.

She didn't know if it was the sexual reference or the fact that she'd hit a bull's-eye, but his eyes went so dark, she couldn't see a trace of blue. Instead, they looked like midnight, intense and unfathomable.

"I was just asking a few questions of a person who fits the stalker profile," was all he said.

"Bullshit."

"I beg your pardon?"

Who knew his sweet Southern drawl could sound so cold.

"You had no reason to ask him any damned thing," she corrected. "Not then. Not there."

"I had reason to suspect him and acted accordingly."

"What reason? What proof?" She would have poked him again except he still held her hand captive.

When he didn't immediately reply, she accused, "You had nothing. Admit it. Your jealousy meter dinged and you pulled on the Macho Man cape and set out to prove you could be a total idiot."

His chin lifted, all pretense at patience and amiability dropping from his face as he straightened to his full height.

Her hand still wrapped in his, he pulled her close. Heat poured through her body. Bending, his face right above hers, he slowly shook his head.

"You think I was jealous of a metro boy with a camera?" he asked in a low growl. "Are you trying to piss me off?"

"I'm not afraid of you," she snapped back. And she wasn't.

God help her, she was totally turned on.

Hot, wet, crazy turned on.

She wanted to dig her fingers into the rock-hard muscles barely concealed by the soft black cotton of his T-shirt.

She wanted to trace her tongue over every inch of him, licking, sucking and biting her way to ecstasy.

She wanted to toss aside all caution, all wisdom. She wanted to give in to the desire that made her toss and turn in her bed at night, a sweaty tangle of lonely limbs.

She wanted being with him not to be the biggest mistake of her life.

But she knew better. He was the kind of guy who wouldn't stop at quick and easy sex. He'd poke and prod, pushing her doors open, forcing her emotions into the equation.

He'd break her heart.

"Macho Man cape?" he muttered quietly. His eyes held hers captive, the intense sexual heat sparking between them dangerously. But it was the humor in them, the easy appreciation of her wit, that broke through her defenses.

It scared the hell out of her. It turned her on like crazy.

No question about it. Reece was the worst thing in the world for her. But dammit, sometimes the worst things felt the best.

"If the attitude fits," she returned softly, her voice dropping to match his in tone and sexual innuendo.

"I'll admit to having a mighty huge…attitude," he said as he pressed her hand flat to his chest. Sierra's fingers curled in pleasure, and she was unable to stop herself from smoothing the soft cotton over the hard, warm expanse of well-muscled flesh.

"Did you want to feel it?" he offered, sliding his other hand down her back to pull her flush against his body.

She could already feel it, pressing in all its hardening glory against her belly. Sierra's knees went weak, excitement swirling in her belly. Damn, he wasn't kidding about huge. But she'd already known that. A fact that kept her awake many a night remembering the pleasure of his long, hard strokes.

"I'd be crazy to get anywhere near your huge…attitude," she declared, as much in final warning to herself as in denial of his offer.

"A little crazy never hurt anyone," he whispered just before he took her mouth with his. Sierra braced herself for the passion, the intense sexual rush. But he tricked her.

His kiss was oh so slow, just the softest brush of his lips over hers. A gentle trace of his tongue, the sweet slide of temptation.

It was that sweetness that snuck beneath her defenses and decided her fate. Unable to stop herself, Sierra curved her hand around the back of his neck, her fingers tangling in the silken strands of hair. She pulled him tighter to her, holding on as she opened herself to his gentle persuasion.

Tongues tangled, lips melted together. Sierra floated on a sea of sensation as the kiss deepened. Like being in a subtle whirlpool, she didn't notice herself being pulled in, pulled down. She barely noticed the building tension, the sexual heat smoldering between her legs.

All she focused on was Reece's mouth and how incredible it felt. One hand behind his head, keeping him from getting away, the other smoothing small, gentle circles over his chest. As he pulled her tighter, she slid her hand to the right. His nipple poked her palm.

She tweaked it, just the flick of her nail over the turgid flesh. Reece groaned and placed his hand against the small of her back, pulling her tighter against his rigid zipper.

It was as if he'd pressed a switch, flipping her from passive to aggressive. Sierra's breath quickened. Using both hands, she reached down to tug his T-shirt from his jeans, then touched her fingers to his bare belly.

Yum. Hard, warm skin with just a light dusting of hair to trail her nails over. She followed the soft hair up his chest, tangling her fingers through the denser curls between his pecs.

Then she got serious. With a quick growl, she wrapped one leg around his calf to pull him closer and at the same time she flicked her fingernails over his nipples.

Their kiss turned voracious. Nibbles turned to nips, teeth and lips and tongues battling for control. Wanting, needing to win, Sierra pressed closer, her ankle hooking around the back of Reece's calf, sliding up and down to mimic the thrusts of their tongues.

His hands moved from the small of her back to cup her butt cheeks, pulling her tighter, closer. So close that she rode his hard thigh, rubbing her swollen nether lips against him in a steady, concentrated pace to coax and build the passion curling low in her belly.

With one large, strong hand still holding her butt, he slid the other down her thigh to the edge of her skirt. Their position made it impossible for him to slide his hand any higher than her knee, though. Frustrated, Sierra dropped her leg to the floor. The move made him release his hold on her. She used the freedom to push the T-shirt up and over his head.

Breathless, needing a moment, she stepped back to give herself a clear, unimpeded view of the delicious sight in front of her.

"Damn," she breathed. Rock-solid male perfection. His shoulders were broad and muscled, his biceps firm and sculpted. His chest was well defined, but not overexercised, and the man had the most delicious, tongue-inviting six-pack she'd ever seen.

She needed to touch it. To taste it. To feel it against her naked skin.

"You're gorgeous," she said, making a twirling motion with her finger so she could get a three-sixty view. Reece rolled his eyes but obliged by turning slowly. He clearly knew his way around the weight room. She had to bite back her moan of approval. His ego didn't need the extra strokes, although her fingers itched to stroke a few other things.

"My body is as much a tool in my job as my computer or a weapon. I work out to stay in shape." He gave a shrug as he faced her again. Obviously not as interested as she was in talking about his sexy body, he reached for her and tried to pull her back against him.

Sierra let him. As soon as she was within distance, she snuggled her face against the hard planes of his chest, her hands curved over his biceps, and gave a purr.

His hands smoothed over her hips, over the curve of her waist and up until he could cup her breasts. She purred again and pressed her thighs tight together. Her own juices, hot and sticky, dampened her curls impatiently.

She needed more.

She wanted it now. She didn't give a damn that they were in her office in the middle of a workday.

"Door?" she gasped against his bare chest.

"Locked," he returned as he slipped his hand under her skirt. She kept her eyes closed, her entire focus on the delectable sensations he was creating in her body. She widened her stance, making it easier for him to reach the center of both their pleasure.

Reece's fingers brushed her wet lips. His growl made her smile. She'd had to dress so conservatively for the event, she'd indulged herself with French-cut silk stockings and no underwear. Apparently she was indulging him with her little secret now, too. It was a secret he liked. She could tell from the immense pressure of his dick against her thigh.

He traced his finger along her wet, swollen lips, making her groan this time. With a wiggle, she tried to entice him closer, but like he did with everything, he set his own pace.

A pace that was quickly driving Sierra crazy. Held against his chest like she was, she couldn't see what he was doing, nor could she see his face. All she could do was feel.

And she wasn't feeling nearly enough.

A little voice in the back of her head screamed a warning, but Sierra promised herself this one treat. Like bribing a recalcitrant child, she offered it up as a reward. As long as she kept complete control, she could look, touch and taste all she wanted.

Always sexually adventurous, she gave herself over to every control fantasy she'd ever had. Control was vital right now, so she might as well make the most of it.

Sierra pulled out of Reece's embrace. Growling in protest, he made a grab for her. She shook her head and put one finger to his lips to silence his objection.

Leaving her skirt bunched around her hips so he could feast his eyes on the wet curls he'd only teased but not really enjoyed, she took a deep breath and drew back her shoulders. His hooded gaze met hers, then, as her hands reached up to cup her breasts, dropped to follow her movements.

The heavy cotton of her blouse, worn specifically to hide any reaction to a stray breeze today, was in the way. Even though she could feel the pressure of her fingers tweaking her nipples through the fabric, Reece couldn't see it.

And she needed him to see. She wanted all his senses fully engaged.

Sight.

Sierra put every bit of body language she had into the act of unbuttoning her blouse. Slow enough to entice, fast enough to excite, she slipped the tiny pearl beads from their holes until she reached her waist. She didn't pull the tail of her shirt out of her skirt. Instead she tugged open her shirt and cupped her hands over her breasts in offering.

Reece reached out as if to take the offer, but she just grinned and shook her head. As if asking him if it were what he wanted, she raised a brow and traced her fingers over the silky edging of her white lace bra.

Reece's Adam's apple bobbed as he swallowed, then fisting his hands at his side, he nodded.

Eyes hooded, she looked down to watch the play of her pale pink nails over her tanned skin and lacy lingerie. Giving herself over to the power of the moment, she tugged the lace down and cupped her bra beneath her breasts, hiking the soft flesh high.

"Oh, sweetheart," Reece breathed as he took in the sight of her deep rose nipples, pouting enticingly and surrounded by white lace.

Sound.

She swirled her index fingers over her already swollen nipples and gave a breathy moan.

"You know what I wish?" she asked softly. Before he could respond, she continued in that same quiet, sexy tone, "I wish it were your fingers rubbing my nipples. Touching me, turning me on."

Smell.

Giving in to the need, she dropped one hand between her legs and rubbed the swollen flesh. Her juices, sticky and sweet, dewed her fingers. The musky scent of her desire filled the room. She saw his nose twitch, his hands flex as he tried to maintain control.

Almost there.

Taste.

She leaned forward and brushed her fingers, still wet, over Reece's lips. He sucked her fingers into his mouth, swirling his tongue over her flesh as he lapped up her flavor.

The feel of his mouth made her even wetter. Sierra squirmed, needing more. Needing to drive him crazy before she gave in to the desperate desire pounding inside her.

With that in mind, she finally, thank God, got to *touch*.

She led Reece over to the desk. Arching one brow, he put his hand on his hat as if to take it off, but she shook her head.

"Keep the hat," she instructed. "But you can lose the pants."

Reece's grin was fast and tight. He arched one brow and put his hand on his belt. Sierra rolled her eyes and shook her head again.

"I'm capable of unwrapping my own treat, thank you," she said with a saucy smile. Pushing him back on the desk, she stood between his legs. As she unbuckled his belt, the back of her hand rubbed teasingly over his rigid length where it pressed against his zipper.

"Can I join in the fun?" he asked.

She shot him a look, letting him know just how unsubservient she knew him to be. Then she arched one brow and unsnapped his jeans. The zipper, with such great pressure behind it, slid open on its own.

"You go ahead and see if you can keep up," she teased.

Knowing he'd take it for the challenge it was, Sierra set out to prove herself the winner in this little game.

And a game it was. One, she admitted in the quiet part of her mind, that she was playing with herself more than with Reece. A game of fire. Telling herself as long as she maintained control, as long as she kept it on her terms, getting burned wasn't gonna happen.

A game of lies.

As his dick sprang free of his jeans and boxers, Sierra eyed the smooth, velvety flesh and told herself she didn't care. Lies were a small enough price to pay for the pleasure she was about to have.

As if hearing her thoughts, Reece curved his fingers over her aching breasts, squeezing, molding and caressing the flesh. He flicked her nipples, tugging the pebbled flesh with a twisting motion. It was as if an electrical current shot between her nipples and her heated core, sparking fire between her legs. Sierra pressed her thighs together and squirmed.

Control. She had to stay in control.

She leaned forward to press her open mouth to Reece's rock-hard belly. The move brought her breasts against his thighs. Sierra shifted, just enough, so her aching nipples grazed over his dick. Reece groaned, his fingers releasing her breasts to tunnel into her hair.

With her mouth, she traced the trail of hair down his belly to his stiff erection. She swirled her tongue over the silken head; then, using both hand and mouth, she set out to blow his mind.

Her mouth played his dick like a fine instrument. Up, down, a swirl here, a suck there. She ignored his suggestions that they make it mutual. She was out for one thing here and one thing only. His complete surrender.

It didn't take long. Sierra found his hot spot, her fingers squeezing the base of his shaft as she sucked hard on the tip. His groans were now in rhythm with her mouth, his hands thrust in her hair.

Swallowing the first drop of pre-come, Sierra quickly shifted so his cock pressed against her breasts. She lifted her chin, making sure Reece was watching, and molded the lush globes, already emphasized by her bra, around his throbbing flesh. He groaned at the sight.

Knowing it would send him over that final edge, she slid her breasts up and down, flicking her fingers over the pouty pink tips. One flick, two, and Reece gave a guttural shout and threw back his head.

Hot, wet liquid shot across Sierra's chest. Reece's climax triggered a shocking one in her. Even though she'd promised herself she was staying in control, she had to give in to the demand. Wanting, needing more, she dropped one hand between her legs to add to the swirling pressure there and brought herself off as the final spasms of his orgasm shook her chest. Her breath gasped over his belly, her body shaking with the power of her release.

Losing control had never felt so good.

CALL HIM A NEANDERTHAL PIG, but the sight of Sierra on her knees in front of him had stirred every primal sexual instinct Reece had.

Reece leaned back on the hard wood of her desk, his hands still gripping the deliciously smooth flesh of Sierra's ass beneath her bunched up skirt. He let his head fall back and sucked in much-needed air, trying to regulate his breathing.

It was as useless as trying to regulate his heartbeat. Both were going crazy.

She was like a fantasy come true. Wild, uninhibited and totally giving. She made him feel like the only man in the world, the best lover on Earth. She made him want to prove he was both of those things to her.

He wondered if she was willing to go another round here on her desk, this time with his mouth doing all the work. He wanted to taste her, to make her scream with the same kind of mind-numbing, body-clenching orgasm she'd just given him.

And for that, he wanted more than a desk in a populated office. He wanted privacy. Hours and hours of privacy.

"Next time," he murmured with a deep breath as he patted her ass one last time, then reluctantly let her go, "I want to see you naked. Totally, completely naked."

His eyes still closed, he felt her move away. He told himself the cold chill washing over him was simply the loss of her body heat.

"Maybe a bed," he added, continuing his fantasy. "Soft feather pillows and even softer sheets. Give me a horizontal surface with a little cushion to it and we can do this a half-dozen times, easy."

He heard the rustle of fabric and knew she was adjusting her clothes. But she still didn't say anything.

Another deep breath, this one because he knew he was wading back into the battle, and Reece opened his eyes. He let himself snicker at the sight of her office. Papers strewn across the gunmetal carpet, his hat lying upside down on a chair.

Figuring his control was as good as it was going to get, he let his gaze rest on Sierra. Her hair waved wildly around her face, the strands tangled from his fingers. Her eyes were hooded, lashes making black sweeps across her flushed cheeks.

And her mouth. Oh, God, that mouth. Swollen and red, her bottom lip still glistened in tempting reminder of the pleasure she'd given him.

She'd used tissues to clean off her chest and was adjusting her bra back into place. Deep rose nipples pushed against the white lace as if mocking him. His jaw tensed, dick jumping back to life as he watched her pull the fabric together and slide the tiny buttons into their holes.

God, it was killing him. He was only allowed that brief glimpse of paradise before she denied him. He wasn't exactly an expert at body language, but the way he was reading things, they were done for this little session.

"Thanks for the offer, but I've had enough…attitude for now," she said quietly.

Anger flashed at her easy dismissal. What kind of game was she playing here? Then, his pissiness dimmed a little as he got a good look at her face. Her mask, usually an ode to sophisticated perfection, wasn't quite in place. He could peek around the edge and see the vulnerability, the fear. He'd seen it once before, when she'd spoken about the stalker pictures and what was at stake.

That she'd feel just as threatened by sex between the two of them was food for thought.

And enough to keep his mouth shut and his attitude to himself. For now.

6

NOTHING LIKE HAVING a woman blow your head off, sexually speaking, then two days later pretend you didn't exist. Reece watched Sierra work the art gallery crowd. She wore some little lacy black dress that reminded him of lingerie with its silky straps and short skirt. Her long, tanned legs went on for miles, all the way to the sexiest pair of do-me heels he'd ever wanted to feel pressed against his throbbing—

"Hey, Reece."

Grateful to have his little fantasy interrupted before it got publicly embarrassing, he turned to face his pretty cousin-to-be. Apparently Belle was the angel to Sierra's devil tonight, her dress a frothy white number that brought to mind Marilyn Monroe. Grateful for something to do, he followed her pseudo perusal of the art exhibit. They slowly circled the room. Fine by him. He got a good three-sixty view of Sierra this way.

"Did you and Sierra pick your colors to match the photographs?" Reece teased.

Tristan DeLaSandro's black-and-white pictures were mounted on the walls and displayed around the room. Interspersed among the photos were bronze sculptures, blown glass bubbles and a really weird something in the middle of the room made from, as far as Reece could tell, empty toilet paper tubes.

"Aren't you the observant one," Belle noted with a playful swat on his forearm. She stopped and glanced around the room, beaming. "Isn't this a great success? Not only is it fab for Tristan's rep, but this kind of press is going to skyrocket his prices."

"Won't that hurt Eventfully Yours?"

"Nah." She shook her head, surveying the crowd as if she were looking for someone. "We've got him under contract. Sierra figured it out a while ago. It's like a double back-patting thing. We support his successful climb up the ladder, and he, in turn, gets regular work from us between rungs."

Impressed, Reece glanced over at Sierra again. Now she'd pulled some guy into a little flirtation. He looked ready to hyperventilate when she laughed up at him. Poor schmuck. He looked like a sad puppy in a bad-fitting tux.

"Why do people feel the need to dress so fancy to gawk at a bunch of naked bodies?" he asked Belle with a grimace. He hated playing dress-up.

Reluctantly following the women's mandate, he'd gone formal. It wasn't the tux that bothered him, though. It was being hatless. Not having planned for fancy occasions on this trip, he'd left his own tux and dress hat in his closet at home. And while a man could wear a pair of rented pants when the situation demanded, a hat was just too personal a thing. Which left him feeling as if his head were naked and in dire need of a haircut.

Glancing over at Sierra, he noted the schmuck was now staring at her as if hypnotized.

"Who's the kid?" Reece asked, unable to stop himself. As soon as the words were out he regretted them.

Mitch, whom Belle had just waved over, joined them, and Reece's regret turned to mocking resignation.

"Kid?" Mitch asked. "This show is nothing short of an R rating. I hope there aren't any kids in here."

Belle laughed up at her fiancé, the look of love on her face making Reece uncomfortable. It was like watching someone with a terminal disease and feeling hopeless to help them.

"Reece means Toby, I think," she said. She gestured to Sierra and her entourage, then raised a brow in question. "Right?"

"Sure," Reece said, shoving his hands in his front pockets. Mitch's hands were plenty busy rubbing up and down Belle's naked back.

"Toby is Tristan's assistant," she explained, tucking her arm into Mitch's and pulling him close. "He handles the bookings, schedules, that kind of thing."

"Hangs out at photo sessions to see the naked women?" Mitch teased, his fingers playing in his fiancée's curls.

"He wants to be a photographer?" Reece asked absently, focused more on the fifth guy to now join the mob around Sierra than on the conversation.

"I think so," Belle answered, just as distracted. But her attention was on the man she was making flirty eyes at, Reece noted with an indulgent grin.

"Or maybe he just likes to see naked women," Mitch said.

"Toby's not into women. But even if he was, there's nothing wrong with that," Belle said. "Being naked, I mean."

Mitch's grin was fast and wicked. And a sign for Reece to leave before he heard his cousin's response.

"I'm going to get a drink," he told the couple, wanting to give them privacy and desperately needing to get away before they started spouting lovey-dovey words.

Reece wandered through the crowd. He didn't know a damned thing about art, but the buzz seemed to be positive. Point and shoot was obviously not in these people's vocabulary.

"Champagne?" asked a roving server, a sexy little redhead poured into a modified tuxedo.

Reece gave her a wink and shook his head, "Beer would go down better. Any chance of getting one?"

"For you, anything," she promised with a look that told him

he could follow her to the kitchen and have it up self-serve, no waiting.

Reece just smiled, though, and murmured his thanks. For all his sexual awareness, understandable given the evening's subject matter, he was here to do a job.

Protecting Sierra was his priority. Not that she was making it easy for him. Her tantrum and adamant denial that the photographer could have anything to do with the stalking had slowed Reece's investigation a little. Not halted it, by any means. But the questions he needed answered were easier when asked directly, which was not an option.

But he had plenty of other ways to find out what he needed to know. He wandered past a picture of a woman in a shower that made him stop and give the artist silent credit. The problem was, the guy was almost too obvious.

Sierra's conviction that the photographer who specialized in erotic art could not be her stalker hadn't stopped Reece from investigating Tristan. Other than the fact that the guy had gone to a ritzy coed boarding school with Sierra and Belle, came from the same filthy-rich background as the women and was estranged from his family, he came up squeaky-clean. As did all the Family executives, Sierra's employees and major competitors.

Frustrated with his lack of progress, Reece had dug in a different direction. Sierra's.

And hit pay dirt.

He hadn't been able to break into her sealed juvie record. But oddly enough, the legal steps she'd taken at sixteen to be declared emancipated from her aunt and uncle's control on the grounds of inappropriate behavior hadn't been sealed. Nor had the paperwork immediately following when she'd taken responsibility for her trust fund at eighteen.

Unfortunately, that and a few hints that she was now hurting for money were all he'd found. Not nearly enough information. He'd have to get the whole story from Sierra somehow.

"Aren't you the naughty boy."

Reece turned at the words and offered his beer-toting waitress a grin.

"Me? Nah, I'm just a man appreciating fine art."

The gal flicked a glance at the shower scene, then back at him. "I meant that you didn't stay where I'd left you. While I was looking for you I had three other guys asking for the same thing I offered you."

Before he could come back with a reply, he spied Sierra making her way over to them. All thought of flirtation or even liquid refreshment fled his brain at the sight of her.

God, she was gorgeous. And it wasn't just her sexuality, on display to perfection in black lace, but the confidence emanating from her. The assured way she crossed the room, as if she knew half the guys' eyes were on her ass. And from the swing of her hips and lift of her chin, she knew perfectly well that her ass was worth the stares.

The redhead sidled closer and gave him a nudge. She held out the tray with the beer on it, her other hand sliding up and down the neck of the bottle in an obvious message.

Reece smirked at the contrast. God bless tacky and obvious. He wasn't interested, but it was a refreshing change from the cold, amused perfection of the woman heading his way.

Speaking of…

"Hello, sweetheart."

"Reece," Sierra greeted with her work smile.

He'd learned the difference now. Her work smile was friendly, but didn't reach her eyes. Her sarcastic smile, the one she usually granted him, was wicked and naughty. And her real smile? He'd seen it offered to Belle, even to Mitch. It put her heart in her eyes.

He wanted that smile for himself someday. And didn't that make him quite the schmuck for wishing?

"They might want to do a better job screening their wait-staff," Sierra muttered as the waitress, seeing Sierra wasn't going to leave, shoved the beer at Reece before sighing and slinking away.

"Jealous?" Reece asked, delighted to see any trace of interest from Sierra. He wouldn't admit it under threat of a hot cattle prod, but his ego was feeling mighty bruised at her decided lack of attention. Not that he expected a woman to fall all over him. But damn, she'd done things to his body that made him hard just remembering.

"Why would I be jealous?" she asked, humor dancing in her blue eyes as she looked directly at him for the first time that evening. The impact of that look hit Reece like a velvet-gloved slap on his butt. Pure temptation. "Unlike some people, I don't need my—what was it?—attitude stroked to feel confident in my sexual prowess."

"Tell me about it," he said, stepping closer. Just enough to tempt himself with the warmth of her body. "You have plenty of little boys panting around you, all more than willing to write tacky poetry to the glory of your attitude."

Sierra's grin—a real one—flashed. The impact of that look sent a shaft of heat straight through his body. Then she got control again and gave him a pitying sigh and an eye roll.

He loved how often he was breaking through that wall of hers now. Two months ago, he'd wondered if her cold demeanor was really who she was. But now he knew better. He also knew all it would take were a few well-chosen taunts to make her lose control. And when she lost control, he got lucky. Every single time.

"Now that's mature. You know, younger men have a lot to offer besides their poetry."

"Their cocky attitudes?" he suggested, giving in to the temptation and running his index finger over the silky skin of her shoulder. She narrowed her eyes, but didn't shift away.

"Exactly," she said, her voice a little breathless. Good. He'd hate to be the only one getting turned on here.

Testing, he slid the edge of his finger up the side of her throat, tracing her jawline. She swallowed and tilted her head, just a little, to give him better access.

A sudden uproar by the door caught their attention. Reece bit back a growl and automatically placed himself between the door and Sierra, angling his shoulders so she was protected. Tristan arrived with a slew of pouting beauties hanging off his arms. The four women together wore less lace than Sierra's entire dress. Reece glanced at the photo display, then back at the women and realized they were the models.

"Now *he* can hold his own," she teased Reece, seeming glad to break the intimate connection he'd been working toward.

"And you'd know this from personal experience?" Reece asked. And yes, he knew damned well he sounded like a jealous idiot. If he didn't, Sierra's smirk would have confirmed it.

"Wondering how big his attitude is?" she taunted.

"He could very easily be your stalker," Reece returned, even though he didn't believe it. Again, it was too obvious.

"I told you it's not Tristan," she said as she sent the man in question a little wave of her fingers.

"No? Has he ever tried to get you naked?"

"He rarely has to try to get any woman naked. He oozes this charm that makes most women start stripping the moment they meet him. I've known Tristan since we were teenagers, and believe me, if his smoldering bad-boy looks don't get them, the soulful sensitivity in that sexy voice of his does."

Reece frowned. Sexy voice? Smoldering looks? He resisted the urge to peer at his reflection in the blown glass bubble. But he did straighten his shoulders and remind himself that he was a perfect shot and could run a mile in four minutes and thirty seconds.

He sneered at metro boy. Bet that guy couldn't hit the side of a barn with buckshot.

"Is that what does it for you?" he asked. He mentally rolled his eyes and called himself a wuss. But he didn't try to take the words back. "Pretty-boy seduction?"

Sierra's gaze lingered on Tristan for a second, as if she were considering. Then she gave Reece a long, amused look.

"Let's put it this way," she finally said. "I'm not into crowds."

"Meaning?"

"Meaning Tristan isn't big on monogamy. He's out to have a good time. In his own words, to experience as much of the delicious bounty that life offers as he can."

"And you have an issue with that?"

"I don't share," Sierra stated with a shrug. "But it's never been an issue since Tristan isn't interested in me."

"Hmm," was all Reece said.

"I'm telling you this to prove my point," she returned impatiently. She broke her unspoken no-contact rule and pressed her hand to his shoulder to make sure she had his full attention. She looked as if she regretted the touch immediately. But she didn't pull her hand away. Instead she leaned in closer and insisted in a quiet hiss, "It can't be him. It just doesn't make sense. He has no motive at all."

"Rejection?"

"I didn't reject him. We're friends."

"Don't fool yourself," Reece told her. "You might think friends, but you're a gorgeous woman and he's not blind or stupid. He'd be crazy to think of you as just a friend."

Her eyes sparkled at the gorgeous comment, but she still shook her head.

"If he's interested, he'd make a move. He's that kind of guy. He isn't, he hasn't. End of story."

"Don't fool yourself," Reece repeated.

"Okay, let's say you're right. Tristan, a confident guy with a healthy sex life, has the secret hots for me. Instead of asking me out, he decides to send me crappy pictures that are so far below his photographic standards he has to force himself to create them blindfolded. Then, to up the stakes, he decides to ruin a lucrative contract that is as vital to his income as it is to my business." She paused to take a sip of her champagne, then wrinkled her nose at him. "All for what? To impress me into sleeping with him?"

"Works for me. You ever want a job in security, I'd take you on." He smiled at her. "That's a good summary."

"You're ridiculous," she decided with a rueful laugh. "You go ahead and think what you want. It's probably moot, anyhow. No pictures have arrived this week. I'm sure the creep has shifted his focus elsewhere."

True. There had been no more photos. Belle had mentioned how relieved she was. Reece, though, didn't share the ladies' optimism.

"Or he's working on a plan to up the stakes," he said before he could censor his words.

The color drained from her face. Sierra's eyes flashed fear, then went cool. "Leave it to you to find the dark cloud."

"Eeyore is my middle name." But he risked losing a limb and smoothed his hand down her arm in reassurance. For the first time, he wasn't thinking sex when he had his hands on her body.

"Doesn't it get old having someone nail that tail to your ass?"

Instead of biting off his hand, she curled her fingers into it when he reached her wrist.

Just for a second, as if absorbing a little strength. Then she let go. Her eyes, blue and intense, dared him to make a big deal of it.

As if. Reece might hug this moment to himself in private, like a contraband teddy bear. But he wasn't stupid enough to ruin it.

"No more than it does having someone hike that chip up onto your shoulder," he said, knowing she'd want the dig rather than sympathy.

"The chip is a part of my spine. It keeps my posture in line." Her words were sassy, her eyes grateful.

Reece felt like freaking Prince Charming. His ego and, as she gave him a warm—real—smile, other pertinent parts of his body swelled appreciably.

Before he could control his response, though, her gaze shifted over his shoulder. Her eyes, so soft and warm for him just a second ago, lit up like freaking Christmas lights. He frowned and glanced in the same direction.

Tristan had apparently caught her eye. The photographer looked as if he was being interviewed, but he lifted a glass of champagne Sierra's way and winked.

Sierra waved at the guy. One of those little finger wiggle things women did that spoke comfort and, quite possibly, flirtation.

He growled low in his throat. Nobody was taking his damned teddy bear.

Grabbing Sierra's hand, the one she'd been wiggling, he tugged her into a corner.

"Hey," she protested.

"We need to talk." He found a private space right between the eight-foot bronze vagina and the Warhol-inspired breast montage.

But as soon as he had her in the pseudo privacy of the corner, all thought of conversation fled. She stared up at him, wide-eyed, with that luscious lower lip of hers damp and inviting.

All Reece could think was how good she tasted. Frustration, now as familiar as his Stetson, pounded at him. There was nothing—no one—he'd ever wanted more in his life. He just had to figure out how he was going to get her.

THE CHAMPAGNE swirled in her head, dulling the rational voice that usually kept Sierra's wilder impulses in line.

"You shouldn't encourage him," Reece said as he crowded her into the corner with the long, hard warmth of his body.

"You're just jealous," she returned, struggling to keep her smile haughty and amused, despite the lust wending its way through her system. All it took was the touch of his hand, the heat of his body, to send rational thought straight out of her head and replace it with a combination of desire and dreams. The desire she could handle. The dreams terrified her. Especially when little comments about being jealous sparked a crazy flame of hope in her, making her wish for more between them than acrimonious attraction.

"What if I am," he admitted.

Shock was the only reason her smile didn't fall away. She couldn't move as she stared up at him. Her first sight of Reece tonight had taken her breath away. Gone was her sexy cowboy and sparring partner. Urbane, smooth and sophisticated, he was gorgeous enough to be one of the male models floating around the show. Except his confidence was something no pretty boy could ever manage. Reece Carter was pure, male strength and he knew it.

But her fascination with him scared her. So she'd deliberately avoided getting near him until she had a grip on her body's reaction to his gorgeous shoulders wrapped in the designer tuxedo.

It had nothing to do with any freakish shyness over their last encounter. She was a strong woman. A sexual being who had no shame in exploring that sexuality appropriately. And there was nothing inappropriate about going down on a single, attractive man who had loved every second of it.

Especially now. The pictures had stopped. Which lent credence to her suspicion that the stalker was someone from her past just trying to stir up misery and stress. Reece would be leaving soon, going back to riding the range or whatever cowboy thing he did on his Kentucky ranch. If she wanted to live out all the sexual fantasies she'd been nursing over the past couple days, she'd better grab the opportunity now.

That wasn't stupid, she promised herself. That was taking control of potentially the best sex of her life.

Sierra glanced at Reece's face and saw the heated interest there. She moved her hip just a little and felt the hard pressure of his erection against her thigh. If she took a deep breath, her breasts, while admittedly not as colorful as the ones surrounding them, would have the thrill of pressing against his chest.

A zing of sexual energy zipping happily through her body, she stared up into his eyes and wanted nothing more than to wrap her leg around his thigh and pull him against her. Just imagining the pressure made her wet and ready.

"I don't mind a little competition," Reece went on, obviously still hooked on the jealousy thing. "But I should warn you, I only play to win."

"Risky," she said softly. "In most games, there is only one winner."

And she knew if she gave in, it wouldn't be her. But she couldn't deny the delicious temptation nudging her thigh, or the insistent answering throb deep in her belly.

"Sometimes winning is about making sure the opponent gets exactly what he wants."

"Sometimes the opponent holds all the cards and intends to win herself."

"If the stakes are high enough, it's worth the risk."

Trying to separate her thoughts from the lust threatening to overtake her, Sierra focused on what was at stake. Then she considered what the game would entail. She convinced herself she was shoving her emotions aside and making this a premeditated decision. That made her smart and looking out for her own interests, not infatuated. After all, this sexual frustration was severely impeding her ability to give one hundred percent to her job or anything else that mattered.

So in a way, playing the game was in her best interest. And wasn't justification a beautiful thing? She mocked herself even as she made the decision.

"Let's go," she decided, taking his hand.

"Where?"

"To ante up for the next round."

ANTICIPATION AND DESIRE had reached a fevered pitch in her belly by the time they arrived at her condo. Other than confirming the address already programmed into his GPS, they'd been silent on the short drive over. Sierra took a deep breath as Reece parked in her driveway and then, not wanting to waste any time with teasing, conversation or even hot car foreplay, she flicked the handle of the Corvette and let herself out.

"In a hurry?" he teased as he joined her at the walkway leading up to her door. The rich scent of jasmine filled the air and the stars seemed to twinkle their own impatience.

"I'm afraid I might have forgotten to feed my cat," she lied dryly. "You know how they get when they want food."

"Never let it be said that I willingly let a pussy go hungry," he deadpanned.

Sierra's laughter rang out in the warm night air. For the first time in her life, she was giving in to the moment. Ignoring her normal cautions and fears, she reveled in the pleasure of being with Reece. In knowing what was coming next. She grinned and tucked her arm into his to pull him toward the door.

"What the hell?" Reece muttered as they reached the front step.

The security lamp bathed the door in dim light. Sierra squinted, trying to figure out what had upset Reece. She stepped closer. A knife protruded from the weathered black ironwood, anchoring a photograph to the door.

Revulsion and fear turned her blood to ice. Ashamed that her hand was shaking, but unable to stop it, Sierra reached out to remove the horror. Before she could touch the knife hilt, Reece's hand shot out, enfolding her fingers and pulling her back.

Holding her tight against him, he wrapped one arm around her shoulder. With the other he punched a button, then held his cell phone to his ear.

"I'm calling to report a criminal threat to cause bodily harm."

7

SIERRA SAT in the pseudo haven of her living room, breathing deep and letting the mellow earth tones relax her. She forced herself to focus on the room and not the conversation in the foyer. She'd painted the walls a deep gold the year before and loved how, at night with the lights low, they made the large open space cozy and warm. Pillows were strewn on every surface. Not so much for decoration, but because when she was home, in her safe place, she loved to sink into their softness and totally relax.

She rubbed her palm in circles over the buttery leather of her sofa and sighed. So much for safe havens.

No. She wasn't letting some perv ruin her hard-won peace. She'd busted her ass to afford this condo, then to decorate it just right. She'd scrimped and saved for it. Just like she'd worked her butt off with Eventfully Yours. Nobody was taking either of them away from her.

But, she reminded herself as she punched her fist into the smooth suede pillow on her lap, the perv had stopped at the front door. So her haven was still sacred.

And that was what counted here, dammit.

"The cops are gone," Reece said as he came through the arched doorway from the foyer. "The report is filed. I've shown them my credentials and assured them we'll be beefing up your security. But they've opened a case. They'll be in touch."

Sierra watched him cross the room, trying to take strength

from his calm demeanor. His voice had been easy, his report to the police simple and to the point. When she'd shaken like a baby, he'd held her hand and continued talking to the cops, unobtrusively taking the focus off her. When the questions had gotten too pointed, he'd suggested she go in the other room while he wound things up. One of the policemen had started to protest, but a simple gesture from Reece had ended that.

Now he stopped across from her, his large body framed between her two teal leather club chairs. The light, so soft and warm against the walls, flicked off his face. And she saw the fury in his eyes.

So much for calm. It was as if he'd channeled every ounce of anger into some small, tight place that could only be seen through his eyes. And the intensity of the anger there was a little scary. Almost scarier than the fact that the perv had stood right out there on her front porch and delivered his hate-filled message with a knife.

Except Reece's anger was for her. In defense of her. To protect her. As if he'd slay dragons for her or something. Sierra shivered. Who knew she'd end up with a white knight fetish?

The idea of Reece caring enough to get angry baffled her. She'd never had a man give two damns about her. None had ever offered more than a token argument over any issue. And stand up for her? Yeah, right. Half of them couldn't stand up *to* her. Sierra had always been on her own.

But not with Reece. He took her personality in stride. Hell, he seemed to get off on it. He wasn't intimidated by her independence, her sexuality or her drive for control.

On top of all that, he had such a lovely *attitude*.

She wanted to check out that attitude again. In great, close detail. She wanted to taste it, feel it. Truly experience it this time. Without barriers, without keeping that wall between them.

"Sierra?"

She put her fantasy on temporary hold and shot him a questioning look.

"The police will do their job. I don't want you to worry." Apparently he thought she'd zoned out for an entirely different reason.

"I'm not worried," she told him. "But I do appreciate you handling the cops and taking care of all that. Now they can do whatever they have to do. But I don't need any kind of security upgrade or to answer the same questions a fourth time."

"The cops are taking this seriously now," he told her. "I hope you are, too."

"The knife was a convincing argument," she told him quietly.

Reece winced, the first time he'd shown any vulnerability since he'd called the cops.

"Want me to phone Belle?" he asked. "I don't think there is any danger, but I'd rather you weren't alone tonight."

"I didn't come home planning to sleep with Belle," she snapped.

She knew her tone was unreasonable, but, dammit, she was scared. That picture had been taken tonight at the art exhibit, then digitally manipulated so it looked as if the huge eight-foot bronze statue of the vagina was eating her. Written across the photo in red ink was one word. It was too filthy to even think of, but Sierra was pretty sure it referred to her and not the statue.

It should have been funny. But it wasn't. Her stalker had been at that gallery. The idea sent a shudder of terror through her.

Needing to connect with Reece to feel safe and normal again, she slid to her feet, making the move as sensual as possible. She didn't bother to tug her short skirt down to mid-thigh, instead letting it ride high. Just high enough to hint, to intrigue.

His gaze dropped to her thighs, bare tonight except for a layer of gardenia-scented body oil. Knowing it was a pitiful ploy, but also how effective it was, Sierra stretched her arms overhead, as if she were stiff from sitting and wanted to work out the kinks.

The reality was, she wanted to hold on to all the kink she could get.

"If you don't want Belle to stay," Reece told her in a toneless voice, "I can bunk on the couch."

So much for pitiful ploys.

"What happened to the game you promised?" she asked, stung. "We came here to play. You're backing out?"

Her words taunted, although playing was not her intent any longer. She didn't know where the need came from. She didn't want to label it for fear it would scare her too much to give in to it. But she needed Reece now. Needed the safety of his arms, the strength of his body. She stepped forward, pressing her hand against his chest.

He frowned, shoving a frustrated hand through his hair as he considered her. "I thought the evening's events might have put a damper on your mood," he admitted. "Threats aren't usually a part of my seductive repertoire."

He sighed, and the rigid power of his chest butted against Sierra's hand. She wanted to feel his flesh. To scrape her fingers through the soft hair, to lick his pebbled nipples.

But instead of slipping the button loose so she could rest her cheek against his warm flesh, she just waited. She didn't want to play games this time.

"I don't want to take advantage of you," he admitted quietly. The look of vulnerability and sweet concern in his gaze did what the threats couldn't.

Tears filled Sierra's eyes.

"No," he yelped, jumping as if she had cooties. "No crying. I can't deal with tears."

Her lower lip quivered, but she managed a smile. Used to burying her emotions, she shoved her reaction to his sweetness aside, ignoring the aching in her heart with the promise she'd deal with it later. Much later.

"No tears," she promised. "Just lots and lots of pleasure."

She slid her body against his and splayed her fingers over his chest. His tuxedo jacket had been tossed aside when he'd talked to the cops, and his black tie dangled on either side of his open collar. She could see the pulse hammering away at the base of his throat and took courage from its rapid beat.

She used the tie to pull him down, to hold him within teasing distance of her lips.

"Unless, of course," she murmured as she licked his bottom lip, "you cry out of pleasure."

She felt his smile against her lips as she deepened her teasing tongue action into a hot, openmouthed kiss, intense and wild. She welcomed the heated passion, letting it burn away the icy fear that seemed to constantly envelop her.

His hands curved over her waist, smoothing up to cup her breasts and then down to cup her ass. Up, down. The move teased, tortured. Constantly kept her body on edge, wanting and needing him to settle somewhere, anywhere, so she could focus on the pleasure she knew he'd give.

She gave in to her earlier fantasy and slid the buttons open on his shirt. A hard tug pulled the fabric loose from his waistband. He grunted a little against her mouth, letting her know the friction of the shirt had been interesting for him.

Using her nails, she scraped soft lines from his collarbone down to his belly.

She broke away from his mouth to press kisses along his

jaw, scraping her teeth over his shadowed beard, inhaling the clean scent of his cologne.

Her fingers circled his nipples, then flicked the hardening nubs. She licked her way down his throat. His hands gripped her hips once, tight. Then, bending his knees just a little, he reached down to snag the hem of her skirt. The lace rasped a delicious trail as he lifted the fabric higher and higher up her thighs.

Needing more, she stepped away and took over the job of removing her dress. With a wink, she spun around and pointed over her shoulder at the zipper.

"Please," she murmured.

He slid the fastening down, bending to trail kisses along her spine as he exposed the flesh. Sierra closed her eyes in pleasure. Who knew the back could be such an erogenous zone?

Unzipped now, she slid her dress easily over her head with just a little wiggle of the hips to free the snug fabric. She tossed it on the couch, then turned to face Reece in just a pair of tiny panties and killer heels.

His eyes went opaque.

"You are so damned gorgeous," he said in a tone so low she could barely hear him.

Once again, he smoothed his hands on either side of her now-bare waist. Up. He cupped her breasts, running his thumbs in a quick tease around the areolae. Down. He slid his hands beneath the tiny scraps of fabric covering her ass to squeeze her soft flesh.

Using his grip on her butt, he pulled her close. Sierra shut her eyes and filled her senses with the incredible feeling of her naked flesh against his body. The rasp of his slacks against her bare thighs. The soft brush of hair against her belly. The hard planes of his chest a vivid contrast to the soft flesh of her breasts.

She wiggled, her nipples scraping deliciously over his chest.

Her hips undulated, forcing her wet, aching core against his thigh in supplication. Each gyration twisted the need tighter, winding her up like a spring.

Reece smoothed his hands higher, pressing into the small of her back to keep her tight against his thigh as he edged backward. He shifted so his thigh was firmly between her legs and bent his head to slurp at her pouting nipples. Little openmouthed kisses. First one breast, then the other, all the while using the hands on her back to keep her moving against his thigh.

To keep the pressure building.

She clenched one hand on his waistband, holding on tight. The other she curled over his bicep. The muscle, hard and rounded, flexed each time he massaged against her back. Sierra clenched her thighs around his leg, pressing harder as she undulated. Heat built, intensified as she imagined what it would be like when she finally felt another hard muscle of his flexing.

Sensing she needed more, he released her back and cupped her breasts. Pushing them together, he ran his tongue over both nipples, first one and then the other. He flicked and circled the sensitive tips with his thumbs to intensify the sensation.

Sierra rubbed harder into his thigh, her climax building tight and fast.

He nipped the flesh. She gasped and clenched her legs. He soothed the sensitive nipple with his tongue. She worked her clit harder against his thigh. Her breath came in gasps. Lights swirled behind her eyes and she whimpered with desire.

He released her, moving so fast she barely realized it was happening. Her eyes flew open just in time to see his shirt fly across the room as Reece dropped to his knees in front of her.

He didn't bother to tug her soaked panties down her shaking legs. He just ripped them straight off.

She almost came then and there.

"Your shades are drawn?" he asked against her belly.

The question pulled her out of her passion-induced fog and melted the icy cage around her heart just a little. She knew it wasn't because he was anti-voyeurism. The man had let her go down on him in her office in front of a huge plate-glass window. Nope, this was all about protecting her.

White knight, indeed.

"The shades are drawn," she assured him as she tunneled her fingers through his hair to urge him to get back to the good stuff. "We have complete privacy."

Meow.

Reece jumped. Sierra snickered. "Okay, almost complete privacy."

He shifted on his knees so he could look around her. Sierra twisted at the waist, glancing back as well. "Selina is just saying hi," she told him with a grin.

"Selina?" He squinted at the cat, then looked up at Sierra. "Catwoman?"

She grinned in delight. "You're a comic book fan?"

"Only the Caped Crusader." He eyed the cat as if he was fighting shyness. But the fluffy tabby just meowed again, then jumped off the couch and padded her way to the kitchen.

"Well, if you're going to narrow your focus, you might as well pick the best," she agreed.

"Back to the game?" he asked, splaying his fingers over her cheeks and squeezing the soft flesh.

"Game on," she agreed.

Reece's grin was its own kind of turn-on. Boyishly wicked, he shot her a wink. Then, moving fast, he grabbed half a dozen pillows and tossed them in a pile beside them. He eyed her, standing there naked and damp, and seemed to get an idea. Then he grabbed another few pillows to add to the pile.

"Join me?" he invited, patting the cushioned mountain. Delighted, she did. Dropping to her knees next to him, she let Reece position her on the pillows as if they were a bed. She noticed he'd moved three off to the side.

"What…"

"My move, remember," he reminded with a shake of his head, referring to their game.

Intrigued, turned on and just the tiniest bit nervous, she settled back on the pillows with a sigh. The contrasting textures—cotton, chenille, velour—added a layer of pleasure to her already heightened senses.

Reece shifted so he was at her feet. She arched her foot, preparing to help him remove her strappy black sandal. But instead, he raised it to his mouth and pressed a kiss to the inside of her ankle.

Her eyes blurred a little.

He lifted the other leg and repeated the kiss. Then he set both ankles on his shoulders, one on either side of his neck. Still on his knees, he rose a little, lifting her butt off the pillows. Grabbing the three he'd set aside, he piled them under her hips, so her body was angled upward.

Then he shifted, sliding up so Sierra's feet skimmed down his back. He settled between her legs, his breath warming her damp lips and making her shudder in pleasure.

Anticipation built, tightening deep in her belly, reminding her of the climax she'd almost had five minutes before. Teasing her with the one she wanted to have now.

She couldn't reach him. Could barely brush the tips of her fingers over the top of his head. Reece grinned, letting her know he was perfectly aware how vulnerable that made her.

She squirmed. But the way her body was angled gave him complete control. Complete and total access to do anything he wanted.

And he took full advantage.

Brushing his hands up her sides to cup her breasts, he pinched her nipples gently, then leaned closer.

She felt his breath, warm and moist, wash over her just before his tongue rasped across her swollen lips. Sierra moaned her approval. He added a twist to the pinch, working her nipples at the same time his tongue worked her clit. Sucking, nibbling, lapping her into a state of blind pleasure.

Tension built higher and higher. Her moans grew shorter, louder. Heat swirled, at first smoky and insubstantial, then coalescing. Hotter, stronger, tighter.

Oh, God. His tongue speared deep inside her, mimicking sex as he moved in and out. Swirling faster and faster. She writhed in pleasure as the climax exploded. Her scream trailed off in a whimper as the power of her orgasm carried her away. All thought, all sensation disappeared. The only awareness she had was the man between her legs and the deliciously terrifying power he had over her body.

So HARD it hurt to walk, Reece followed the sway of Sierra's naked hips into her bedroom. His fingers itched to grab those hips and press her body between his and the wall. To take her from behind as she stood there, arms above her head and trapped. To make her scream in ecstasy. Again.

Then he stepped through the doorway into her bedroom and forgot his hard-on.

It was straight out of a fantasy. Filmy blue fabric hung from the ceiling, surrounding the bed in a curtain of sensuality. Rich colors, shimmering linens, antique furnishings, they turned the room into a sultan's harem.

"Wow," he breathed, feeling like a juvenile but unable to help himself.

"What?" she asked in a defensive tone. "You don't think I'm girly enough for such a feminine room?"

"Feminine?" Reece slid his gaze over her naked body, the pert breasts and tangle of dark curls screaming female power. "Sweetheart, you are enough everything. I'm just blown away at the pure sensuality of this setup. It's like something out of a fantasy."

For the first time in their acquaintance, Sierra blushed and looked down. He realized he was getting a peek at more than her bedroom. This was a glimpse into the real Sierra. The woman underneath the smart-ass comments and drive for success.

The woman who was starting to fascinate him to the point of stupidity. Not screw-up-on-the-job stupidity, but risk-his-emotions stupidity.

He looked around the boudoir and realized he didn't care. She was worth any amount of stupid. She looked up and he saw the vulnerable pleasure in her gaze. He vowed to spend the rest of the night showing her every kind of pleasure he could. To give her a night of sensual fantasies worthy of this room.

"It is a fantasy, actually." Modesty apparently forgotten, she sidled up beside him and wrapped her arms around him. One lush breast pressed against his arm and her curls, still damp from his tongue and her orgasm, teased his thigh. Reece's erection danced a little, reminding him that he had other things to do than talk. "This room is completely for me. I filled it with all the things that turn me on."

"Sex toys?" he asked, looking around in interest.

"Right," she said with a snicker. "Because my fantasies are so unoriginal and unimaginative."

And didn't that make Reece glad he didn't have sex toys in *his* room?

"Tell me more," he invited, wanting—needing—this peek inside Sierra's complex mind. Every time he thought he had the woman pegged, he discovered another facet. He had a feeling if he spent a hundred years with her, he'd still be fascinated.

Scary thought, so he focused on the next hundred minutes and calculated how many climaxes he could give her to distract himself.

"Tell you why this is a fantasy room?" she clarified.

He gave a half nod, but the climax count had dimmed his curiosity.

Not realizing it, Sierra patted his ass through his slacks, then moved away to glide across the carpet.

"Colors and curtains. I love the way it feels to climax and see the rich colors flashing behind my closed eyes." She lifted the sapphire-hued silky fabric hanging from the ceiling and wrapped it around her naked body. "I close the curtains and feel like I'm in a romance novel. It's romantic and sexy at the same time."

He mourned the loss of her naked body, but his own body reacted instantly to the peekaboo effect of her nipples pressing against the curtain. Seeing where his attention was focused, she ran one hand up the fabric, pressing it tighter to her body. Her fingers caressed her pointed nipple, then she used the curtain to rub over her flesh.

Reece had taken two steps forward before he even realized he'd moved. Holding her eyes with his, he pinched her nipple beneath the curtain. The silky fabric slipped off the peak. Her hiss of pleasure told him she liked the move, so he did it again.

Then, unable to stop himself, he bent his head and sucked her nipple, fabric and all, into his mouth. She mewed with pleasure. He scraped his teeth over the flesh, made even more sensitive by the wet fabric. Pulling back, he blew softly on the damp blue spot and watched her shudder.

Before he could do more, she stepped away. Not in rejection, he knew, since she stopped to pull his mouth down for a wet, tongue-dueling kiss. But because she had more to tell him.

Putting a foot between them, she lifted one of the pillows

off the bed. Velvet with gold rope braided around it and tassels at each corner. She rubbed the fabric over her belly, her eyes half-closed in delight.

"Then there are the fabrics. Velvet, silk, satin. I love the sensation of the different textures on my skin."

She pressed the pillow lower, against her mound. With a soft undulation, her breath shuddered out and she gave him a look that made it clear she'd used this method to pleasure herself plenty of times.

Reece reached out to trace her breast. He didn't touch her nipples, just cupped the weight of her soft globes and watched her use the pillow against her wet folds. He wanted to replace the pillow with his hand, with his tongue. He could still taste her juices. He was starved for more.

Sierra didn't need toys. All the dildos in the world couldn't keep up with this woman's imagination.

"What's your ultimate fantasy?" he asked, vividly reminded of his hard-on pressing insistently against his pants as she indulged herself. If he hadn't already been crazy about her, her words and the images they evoked would have seduced him into insanity.

She gave him a long, seductive look, her lashes a sweep of black over her cheeks as she handed him the pillow. Taking the hint, he pressed it against his erection, his breath shuddering at the contrast of the soft fabric against his straining flesh. Sierra eased herself back on the bed. Her body supported in a half-sitting position by the mounds of pillows, she crooked her finger in invitation.

"My ultimate fantasy? A man who can take all of that and make it better than I imagined."

Reece grinned and tossed the pillow on the foot of the bed. He pushed his already unzipped slacks off his hips and let them fall to the ground before stepping out of them and his boxers. He bent over to grab his wallet, but when he straightened, she was holding a string of wrapped condoms.

His grin, among other things, grew even bigger. Nothing like a woman who believed in preparation. And better yet, he thought as he counted the condoms, in his virility.

"What I'm going to do to you will be better than anything you've ever imagined," he promised. "When I'm through, you won't need fantasies. You'll have memories instead."

8

"YOU MADE ME breakfast?"

Sierra stood in the doorway of her kitchen and stared. She couldn't keep the delighted pleasure out of her voice. Or off her face, judging by how wide her grin felt. But she didn't care.

He'd made her breakfast. Real food, even, not just cereal and milk. Besides a bowl of melon, Sierra spied French toast, bacon and, if her nose didn't deceive her, fried potatoes. Yum.

Her heart, already vulnerable after the night's passion, stuttered. Make that four bouts of passion, she reminded herself as she shifted her bare thighs beneath the tails of his barely buttoned white dress shirt. But she'd never had a guy cook for her before. Granted, she'd never let a guy spend the night before, either.

Nor had she intended to let Reece stick around. But every time she'd thought about booting him out, he'd thought of ways to drive her crazy. Exhausted but well-satisfied, she'd finally fallen asleep at daybreak, draped over his deliciously spent body.

Since it was a Sunday, she'd have automatically slept till noon, but the very yummy scent of food had woken her.

"I hope you don't mind," Reece said.

She eyed him standing there bare chested and poured into a pair of well-worn jeans—where'd they come from, she wondered—with his naked toes peeking out from beneath the ragged hem. His hair was sleep-tousled, his jaw dusky with the night's growth, and he held a spatula in his hand.

"Mind?" she repeated. "Only if you burn the food."

His laugh was fast and wicked. "I cook like I do everything," he assured her. "Damned good."

Sierra gave him a slow, easy smile and stepped forward to trace her hand over his warm, bare chest. "Then this meal should be incredible."

"The best you've ever eaten," he bragged, handing her a plate filled with golden French toast, fried red potatoes and crispy bacon.

Sierra took the plate and gave him a long, considering look. "We'll have to see, won't we?"

No way was she stroking the man's ego. She'd stroked everything else quite nicely, so he didn't need any more.

She swallowed her first mouthful of rich egg-battered bread and gave a moan of pleasure. "The only thing better than this," she told him as she scooped up another bite, "is sex. If you want to do me and feed me both at the same time, it'd be like dying and going to heaven."

She bit into her bacon, the crisp hickory flavor perfect with the maple syrup from the French toast. "Definitely heaven."

"Want coffee?" Reece asked, holding up the carafe.

Her mouth full, she just nodded. God, what a man. He understood great sex, good food and the need for caffeine.

Now this was the way to rock a morning after. And she'd worried it'd be awkward? Oh, not over the sex. She'd figured good sex didn't require blushing, stammering or weirdness the morning after. But that whole pathetic thing about falling apart over the knife? That had been fertile ground for awkwardness.

The memory of the knife, the threat, filled her head. She could barely breathe when the image tried to grab hold of her.

Think of something else, she scolded herself, unwilling to let the fear ruin her morning.

"Do you cook like this all the time?" It was the first thing that came to her mind.

"You mean breakfast for women?"

Sierra opened her mouth to make a smart-ass retort, then snapped it shut as she realized yes, that's exactly what she meant. She suddenly wondered how many women he'd been with. Had any of them mattered emotionally? Mitch had said something once about divorce. Had Reece's heart been broken?

She wanted to hug him close, then grill him for all the details.

Was that cute or pathetic?

She noted the bitter taste in her mouth and a nasty knot twining through her gut as she imagined some woman mattering enough for him to promise his life to her.

Definitely pathetic.

Irritated with herself, she gave him a shrug instead of answering and said, "You do make the best French toast I've ever had."

Reece's lips twitched.

"What're you doing tomorrow night?" he asked, his look telling her he knew she was trying to wriggle off the hook and would allow it. But he was still amused.

Sierra mentally reviewed her calendar. Monday night? "I don't have anything scheduled. We have a team meeting in the afternoon, so I kept the evening open in case it ran late."

"Dinner?"

Sierra slowly lowered her fork, her gaze locked on his. They both knew it was more than a casual request to eat together. So many times in the past he'd asked her on dates. Six years ago, she'd figured it was the simple desire to get in her pants. Two months ago, she'd figured it was probably a desire to repeat their little closet adventure. That and a desire to conquer her. Simple testosterone challenge.

And now? Now it was scary as hell. Because it had nothing to do with the simple equation of sex and everything to do with the messy concept of emotions.

Great sex, like they'd had, required a certain degree of trust. Emotions demanded so much more. They demanded you rip the doors off your soul and let the other person poke and prod and judge.

She noted the easy humor in his eyes, the lack of pressure. He wasn't going to push her. Reece would wait. He obviously figured he had all the time in the world to break her down.

Did she have it in her? The trust, the emotions, the *more?*

Her stomach pitched, terror whispering warnings and threats in the back of her head. But she ignored them all. She wanted— needed—to find out.

"I don't know how late the meeting will run, but dinner afterward sounds good," she told him slowly. As soon as the words were out, she wanted to grab them back. What was she thinking? It'd be so much safer, smarter, to stay locked away from temptation.

But then Reece grinned. That slow, easy smile. One side quirked up higher than the other in that cute way she was learning to count on, and his eyes shone with delight and just a smidge of triumph.

But all he said was, "Great. I'll pick you up at your office. We can do Madeo? Or a light meal and a club?"

Nice, easy dates. The kind that let them stay on the surface and didn't require more commitment than a few hours and basic social skills. The only kind of dating she allowed herself.

In other words, safe.

She looked down at her breakfast, done to perfection. She shifted a little in her chair, the delicious ache from all-night sexual aerobics zinging through her. She looked at Reece, sexy, sweet and so masculine that it made her ovaries hurt.

"Why don't we meet here," she finally suggested. Taking a deep breath, she put it all on the line. "We can relax, cook or order in and just spend some time together. Maybe watch a movie or just—" she sucked in a shuddering breath, but kept her tone light and easy "—you know, get to know each other."

His eyes darkened, deeper even than they'd looked just before he'd climaxed. The intensity, the power there, made her wish she'd just shoved more food in her mouth instead of mentioning a date. Even dating might be too risky with Reece.

Then he reached out and curled his hand around hers. Just for a second, to squeeze it and let go. Then he changed the subject. They talked about the upcoming Family tea, about his business, and his disdain for L.A. He talked about his ranch back in Kentucky, what his life was like there and how much he missed his dad. Sierra listened raptly, even as her brain filed his words away in the warning section.

This was a man who would be leaving soon. Which was for the best, she told herself. And that lump in her stomach was because she wasn't used to eating such a big meal after exerting so much energy.

"I wanted to talk to you about some things," Reece said after he'd polished off all the food on his plate.

Her stomach settling, Sierra eyed the last piece of bacon on the platter and wondered if he'd think she was a pig if she grabbed it before he could. Then she realized the man had done her upside down and sideways, and figured there weren't any secrets left.

So she snapped it up and bit into the delicious done-to-perfection crispness before raising her brow to indicate he could ask away.

"What are the details behind your declaration of emancipation at sixteen? What'd your aunt and uncle do to piss you off?"

The food stuck in her throat. The room did a slow three-sixty, leaving spots in front of Sierra's eyes and a ringing in her ears. Her heart raced but she couldn't find air to breathe.

With effort, she swallowed the bacon, its once delicious texture scratching her dry throat. She blinked a couple times, trying to focus on the wall across from her. The feeling of betrayal was all the worse because she'd trusted him. She'd relaxed her guard and let him in.

She'd been stupid.

Finally, Sierra met his patient stare. She sucked in a deep breath, but her mind was still blank. She wanted to rail at him, to tell him where to get off, to rip him to shreds for opening that door.

But she didn't have any words.

"I think your uncle could be the person behind the stalking," Reece explained, as if that made his betrayal acceptable.

"You think wrong."

He just leaned back in the chair and stared, unfazed by her cold tone.

"Really? Tell me why."

Why what? Why she'd spent her summers with boarding school friends to avoid having to get near the nasty old man who liked to whisper dirty suggestions whenever he cornered her in the hallway? Why she'd spent the first year after her mom's death lying awake at night with the lights on, terrified that if she turned them off, he'd sneak into her room?

Why, when fear had overcome her pride and she'd begged her aunt to protect her, she'd been slapped so hard her cheek had bruised? Why, the last time her uncle had tried to put his hand in her shirt, she'd been arrested for shoving him down the stairs?

The memories, like vicious monsters, attacked her. Biting, scratching to get out and overwhelm her. Sierra forced herself to control the breaths, in and out. To count each inhalation, each exhalation. Years of practice assured her the struggle was private. Nobody, not even Belle, had any idea of the ugliness Sierra kept locked away. And nobody ever would.

Her uncle wasn't behind this. If he was, the filthy pictures would have come with a price tag.

She sucked in one last, focused breath and then pasted a cold expression on her face.

"I'm not telling you a damned thing," she said, unable to keep the bite out of her tone. She pushed away from the table and gracefully slid to her feet. She fisted her hands on hips still covered in his shirt and glared down at the calm curiosity on his face. "You have no business, none, digging into my life and my past. You're here to protect me from some freak with a camera, not to put me under a microscope. Why don't you actually do your job instead of playing at it like you're a ten-year-old with your first magnifying glass and secret decoder ring."

He had the gall to smile. He was, however, cautious enough to set his chair down on all four legs instead of leaning back anymore. "I missed out on the ring," he said. "I did get a cool hat, though."

Too furious to speak, she hissed instead. Her fingers curled into her palms in painful restraint.

His smile fell away and he gave her a shrug. "I am doing my job, Sierra. It's to investigate anybody who might have enough justification in their own ugly mind to threaten you like this."

Instead of pacifying, his words only added to her panic. Knowing she had to leave before the walls closed in on her, she rolled her eyes and gave him a sneer. "First Tristan and now this? You're obviously not as good as you think you are."

With that, she stomped around the table and headed for the door.

Just as her bare toes hit the threshold, he called out, "That's not what you said last night."

She let her finger respond and just kept going.

THE TABBY WOUND in and out of his ankles as Reece watched Sierra storm out of the room. He was oddly comforted.

Now that was the Sierra he knew.

A few knots of tension unraveled from his shoulders. He'd been a little worried after the sweet tenderness of their last little tumble. Afraid she'd been more vulnerable than she'd let on, that maybe she'd given in to that cliché of falling for her protector. But the finger she'd flipped his way as she'd headed out assured him she was no more vulnerable than a she-cat.

As he carried their plates to the sink, he thought of Sierra's reaction to his questions. Fury and fear.

The fury he'd expected. The fear had churned at his gut.

What the hell had happened there? Had they given her a bad time? Nah. He couldn't imagine a woman as strong and together as Sierra putting up with any crap, even as a teenager. From what he'd found out, after her mother's death when she was thirteen she'd gone to live with her mom's superrich sister. At fourteen she'd gone off to boarding school, and from what he could tell, had never spent more than a few weeks with her aunt and uncle again after that.

So what was the story? Reece thought of all the times Shawna had whined that she wished she had a rich relative. She figured the only way for a girl to get herself out of lower-middle-class doom was rich relatives. Or a husband who'd work his ass off.

Had Sierra's issues been over money? Over a sense of entitlement? Rebellion about living in a new home, with new authority figures? Probably a combination.

The blank terror that had flashed so briefly in her eyes nagged at him. Was it something more? He had to know. It was vital to his case, to his protecting her.

At least, that's what he was telling himself.

Because there was definitely a story here. Some kind of

ugliness, and it could damned well be coming back to haunt her in the form of filthy pictures and threats. It was his job to stop it.

So Reece would do whatever he had to in order to get the job done. Including pissing off the most incredible woman he'd ever slept with.

He'd definitely be on his own when it came to investigating her uncle. Contemplating the rest of the mess, Reece rocked back on his heels, his hands shoved in the pockets of the jeans he'd found in the trunk of his Corvette.

Santa Barbara wasn't too far. He glanced out the window. And it was a nice day for a drive.

He checked his watch. If he left now, he could stop by his office and do a little research first. He had to be back for a dinner meeting with Driscol to listen to the guy's last-ditch effort to talk him into considering L.A. as a new home base.

Then he looked at the breakfast dishes. Plates, glasses, a pile of dirty pans. He never had learned to cook without making a mess.

But he figured after five orgasms and French toast, Sierra could do the dishes.

"SIERRA?"

"Hmm?" Sierra tore her gaze from the blank wall to meet Belle's impatient look.

"I was saying I think we're on track with the three parties this week, but we still need to solidify the tea party plans for Family's sponsors and advertisers."

"Right," Sierra agreed.

Belle frowned, her pen tapping an irritated beat against her notebook. "You're not with me here. What's up?"

A delightful stomach-clenching journey into the nightmares of her past? Nah, Sierra didn't much feel like sharing that. It was bad enough that it was in her mind—she wasn't about to put it into words. But ever since Reece had brought the specter of her uncle out of the closet and into the open, she'd been bombarded by memories. None of them pleasant, to say the least.

"Sorry," she apologized. "I'm a little off today."

Belle's frown melted into a worried look. "Are you still thinking of that picture on your door?"

Sierra just shrugged and flicked a piece of imaginary lint from her blue jeans. She wasn't, but it was easier to let Belle run with that than admit the truth.

"Look, it's all going to be fine. Reece is on the job and he told me this morning that he was feeling confident that he'd find out who's behind the threats."

Sure he was. At his current rate of brilliant deductions and shadow jumping, he'd probably accuse the postman next.

Wait.

"This morning?" He'd talked to Belle today? Where? Here? He'd stopped by and what? Ignored *her?* Sierra fought back a growl. Yes, she'd planned to ignore him if he came by. But she had good reason to. He'd been a jerk. But what reason did he have to ignore her?

Her lower lip dangerously close to pouting, Sierra reached into the pocket of her blazer and pulled out a piece of candy from her now-ever-present stash. She grimaced as she popped it into her mouth. Her nerves were so shot lately she'd had to switch to sugar-free. Sugar-free was doing nothing to mellow her out, though.

"Yeah, Reece was in this morning before you arrived," Belle said, unaware of her friend's turmoil. "You might as well know. He comes by every morning. He checks the building security cameras, the mail, that kind of thing."

It was hard to hold on to the sharp edge of irritation while soft, gooey emotions were crashing over her. Sierra tried her damnedest, though. Because while she could admit that Reece had a certain justification for looking into her past, it didn't mean she could get beyond what his kicking that door open had done to her.

Or more precisely, she didn't want to.

"I didn't realize he was that…" What? Protective? Sweet? Thorough? That'd be a lie, since she knew he was all of those. But she'd had no idea he was putting so much effort and time into guarding her and hadn't said a word.

"An ounce of prevention keeps him from having to pound someone into the ground." Belle gave a wink.

Sierra forced a smile and gestured to the huge calendar posted to the wall. "I guess we should be focused on reworking this scheduling snafu, huh?"

Belle gave her a long, searching look. Then she reached into her laptop case and tossed a bag of butterscotch candies on the table with a little shrug. "Fake sugar is bad for you. Besides, you think clearer on butterscotch."

Sierra sucked in a breath, measured the pressure of her waistband against her skin and decided she didn't care. With a grateful smile, she popped a candy and let the sugar soothe her nerves.

For the next hour, the two women juggled their schedules, brainstormed event ideas and lined up vendors. In the second hour, Tristan and Toby arrived, and they shifted focus to Family and their event lineup for the next two weeks.

By hour three, they were in dire need of caffeine. Belle and the guys went to Starbucks. Sierra, feeling a little guilty for her lack of attention during the first half of the meeting, insisted on staying behind to transfer their schedule into the computer.

She was about halfway through when she heard the boardroom door open.

"I hope you brought me a maple scone with my latte," she said as she hit Save. "I'm starved."

"I'd have taken you for more of a cookie kind of gal than a scone fan."

Sierra's fingers froze on the keys as Reece's slow drawl washed over her.

He had the gall to come here? To act as if nothing had happened? She turned just as he reached her side. He leaned forward as if to kiss her hello, but her hiss stopped him short.

His dark brow shot up to meet his cowboy hat. He straightened and rocked back on his heels, shoving his hands into the front pockets of his jeans.

The move drew her attention to the delicious stretch of denim level with her face. Her breath caught as she remembered the delightful talent hidden beneath that zipper.

Then she glanced up and met his eyes. They were guarded, watchful. As if he'd expected her reaction but wasn't going to comment on it. What game was he playing?

"What're you doing here?" she asked as she leaned back in her chair, crossed one knee over the other and folded her arms across her chest. She knew damned well what her body language was saying. And short of throwing her empty coffee mug at him, it was the closest to "Get the hell out!" she could get without letting him win.

"We have a date, remember?"

Her jaw dropped so fast, she was surprised it didn't hit her chest. Oh my God. Talk about audacious.

"You actually think I'm still going out with you?"

"We'd decided to do takeout and movies." His look made it clear that he didn't feel her anger and hand gestures constituted breaking their date.

"But if you'd rather go out, let's make it casual since I don't have a change of clothes," he continued, leaning against the wall and crossing his booted feet at the ankle. Despite his casual pose, his shoulders were set as if he were braced for her argument.

Before she could accommodate him and blast him with every colorful word in her repertoire, the others returned. They stopped short just inside the doorway as if the tension in the air was some kind of powerful force field. The brown paper bag crunched loudly in Toby's hand. Sierra didn't spare him a glance to see why; she was too focused on the other two men.

Tristan's mouth quirked at the corner, amused speculation clear in his black eyes.

Was Reece going to spout more of his ugly accusations at the photographer? Tristan had figured the confrontation at the park had been over jealousy. The only person besides Sierra and Belle who knew of the stalker situation was Corinne. After his rudeness at the picnic, Reece had insisted they keep all information private. Was he about to change that mandate? Sierra held her breath, ready to jump up and defend her friend.

But Reece surprised her. He stepped forward to greet Belle with an easy hug. Then he turned to Tristan and held out his hand. The men shook and, as Sierra stared in shock, launched into easy chitchat while Toby, efficiently invisible as always, unpacked scones, cookies and zucchini bread.

"Reece, we're going to be a little longer," Belle said, taking her bread and chai tea to her seat. "Why don't you have a snack while you wait?"

Sierra almost pelted her with a scone.

As if he had every right to be there, Reece settled into a corner and watched the rest of their meeting. He even interjected a few comments here and there. Hell, he was shoving himself in more than Toby ever did. Sierra wanted to make an issue of that, but she had to be honest. Toby managed the photographer's business, but he was like a computer geek—silent, and easily ignored. So his lack of participation wasn't anything that could be attributed to Reece's big mouth.

As they wound up the meeting, Tristan turned to Reece

and said, "We're gonna grab some food and game time. Want to join us?"

Sierra glared at the photographer. Now that he was not on Family time, he looked more like himself, his black hair spiky, tooled leather and studded bracelet on his wrist. The smiley face on his T-shirt sported a Mohawk and facial piercings.

"Thanks," Reece said. "But I'll have to pass. Sierra and I have plans for the evening."

This was her cue. The perfect opportunity to use the others' presence to buffer her refusal to go out with him. Sierra opened her mouth, but no words came out. Calling herself all kinds of idiot, she snapped her teeth shut.

Reece winked.

She glared.

His grin widened as he tilted his hat to her in acknowledgment of her defeat.

Tristan took the refusal in stride, but gave Sierra a naughty wink and said, "Don't let her get you in trouble. She's hell on wheels with Super Mario Brothers."

Reece's lips quirked but he kept his expression straight. "You're into video games?"

Tristan gathered his portfolio, photographer's loop and grease pen, and grinned. "Dude, I'm all about the games."

He and Reece launched into the pros and cons of various gaming platforms, then slapped hands like old buddies before Tristan offered a goodbye to the room on his way out the door, Toby trailing silently behind.

Belle didn't say anything. She didn't have to. The curiosity was so clear on her face she might as well have written across the white board "Give me all the details" in big, bold red pen.

Sierra ignored her. If she opened her mouth, she knew she was likely to toss out some chicken-ass plea such as asking Belle and Mitch to join them for dinner.

And like the full-sugar butterscotch candies that she knew were so bad for her but she craved like mad, Reece was a temptation she knew she wasn't going to give up easily.

At least, not tonight.

9

HE'D WANTED PIZZA. She'd wanted sushi. They'd settled on burgers. Reece watched Sierra scoop up napkins and a candle. Then she gestured toward the white paper bags in his hand and tilted her head to the French doors off her kitchen.

"Let's eat outside," she said.

Three words. Apparently this was her average for the night. Other than directions to her favorite gourmet burger place, she'd kept every sentence to three words or less.

Reece hated eating outside. Bugs, weeds, wind messing with the food. But he figured he'd pushed his luck enough tonight insisting they keep the date, such as it was. He'd chow down on a few mosquitoes if necessary to get Sierra into a talking frame of mind again.

He waited until she'd stepped out the door before heaving a sigh. Damn, this wasn't the night he'd signed on for. He'd figured she'd have set aside her tantrum by now. After all, it had been two days. Who stayed mad this long over something like a simple question?

Figuring it was worth finding out what exactly her game was, he followed her out the French doors.

He looked around in surprise. A small waterfall cascaded over the rocks at the far end of the diminutive yard. No fence was visible because of the richly scented flowering vines surrounding the perimeter. Huge blooms, rich colors, a riot of hanging plants all gave the space a feeling of lush, tropical growth.

Sierra placed the fat candle in the terra-cotta pot in the center of a little bistro-style table and, without giving him a glance, set out napkins and drinks. He didn't know if it was the prospect of food or the quiet setting, but some of the stiffness had left her shoulders and she seemed to have finally unclenched her jaw.

Whew. Maybe this evening was salvageable. A nice candle-light dinner in a peaceful garden with a gorgeous woman who, he noted as she stepped around the table, had the sweetest ass he'd ever seen in denim.

An ass he couldn't wait to feel cupped in his hands again. Images of her face as she reached a groaning climax filled his mind. Reece's body immediately showed its interest in a repeat performance. He grinned. Or maybe a third.

Feeling good about the evening's prospects, Reece crossed the flagstone and set his bags on the table as she sat down. Sierra didn't say a word. She just took out a cardboard box from the bag, opened it and then, as if just noticing he was standing there, gestured to the chair across from her.

Reece frowned and, refusing the invitation, tucked his hands into the front pockets of his jeans. His dick, already hard and aching, protested the strain of the denim.

"Is this going to be a silent meal?" he asked.

Maybe he'd jumped the fence in his prediction for the evening. Not that he was only interested in revisiting her velvet boudoir. He ignored his dick's twitching protest at the thought. But, dammit, burgers over a cold game of solitaire didn't hold much appeal, either.

"Have a seat," she said without answering directly.

He raised a brow.

"Your food's getting cold."

Four words. Progress.

Apparently not willing to leave hers to the same fate, she bit into her burger. He could smell the combination of sweet grilled pineapple and tangy teriyaki from where he stood.

His brain told him to leave. But some other part of him, he refused to label where, said he'd fumbled his questions the other day and he deserved the attitude she was dishing out.

The question was, which part was gonna call the shots here?

Pineapple juice glistened, just a drop, on her lower lip before she ran her tongue across the soft flesh. She arched a brow and, as if she didn't care one way or the other, swirled a fry in ketchup. She locked her eyes with his and held them as she lifted the potato wedge to her lips and licked the tip.

His eyes focused on her mouth. He could almost taste the salty sweetness. His body hardened at the sight of her tongue, wet and pink. His breath caught as she licked a smidge of red from the corner of her luscious lips.

She snapped the tip of the potato off in a clean, vicious bite.

He narrowed his eyes.

"Promise?" he asked. "Or threat?"

"I haven't decided."

God. He was getting turned on by takeout. Pathetic. An amusing play on her part. He raised his brow to acknowledge her win, and with a smirk, dropped into the chair opposite her and unwrapped his own dinner.

"So, I'm curious…" she said slowly when he was about halfway through the best burger he'd had outside of Kentucky.

Reece waited, wondering if her long pause was to honor the three-word rule or if she was gathering her thoughts.

"Do you ever listen?" she asked.

"Huh?" He let the burger fall back into the box and wiped his fingers on his napkin, using the time to try and figure out what she meant. "I have excellent hearing."

"Right. But do you listen?"

Reece leaned back, letting the chair balance on two legs and gave her a long, contemplating look. "Wanna clarify?"

"I told you Tristan isn't behind the pictures. You ignored me."

He nodded, again acknowledging her point.

"I told you it wasn't anyone from my past."

He didn't have to wait for the next words. "You think I ignored you?"

"Didn't you?" Her tone was neutral. Mellow, even. As if they were discussing the type of flowers she was growing along the fence. "You investigated me. You opened doors I'd locked shut. And you did it after I'd told you not to."

As she threw the last words at him, he saw the first flash of emotion in her eyes since she'd hissed her warning that he back off in her office that afternoon.

It wasn't a pretty emotion, either. Anger mixed with something. He couldn't tell what, but it made his gut ache to see it.

He figured this wasn't the time to mention his attempt to talk to her uncle. He'd ended up having to make do with a very bitter, very nasty aunt.

"So, I'm asking you again. Do you ever listen?"

Almost missing the three-word rule, Reece puffed out his cheeks and tried to figure out the smartest answer. He couldn't find one, though. So he settled on the truth.

"I always listen," he told her. "My job depends on my ability to hear both what people are saying and what they aren't. But I guess you're asking more than that, right?"

She pushed her food away and nodded.

"I don't tend to let others tell me how to think. Or how to do my job. I heard your words—and yes, your warning. But when my instincts, my brain, tell me to do something, I listen to them first."

Her hand reached into the pocket of the light brown jacket

he wore, but after a second she pulled it out empty. Her
lenched fist was white against the black iron table as she
eemed to struggle with something.

Then she met his eyes and asked, "But this isn't just business.
This isn't just some impersonal case. And you invaded my
privacy."

Reece had to acknowledge her point. If he expected her to open
er doors, he had to be willing to let her see into his, he realized.

"Tit for tat, then. I poked into your past, I'll share some of mine
n exchange." He took a deep breath, then sighed. "I was
narried."

Her raised brow indicated that was old news and she was
vaiting to hear why it was relevant. He had to hand it to
Sierra, she didn't make things easy. He found that so damned
exy about her.

"Shawna wasn't a bad lady. She just wasn't right for me. Or,
should say, I wasn't right for her." Reece pulled a face at that
dmission. He'd gone into the marriage looking for a fantasy
woman, he admitted to himself. Looking for a replacement for
he woman across from him. Which was why this time, he was
letermined to stick it out with Sierra. To figure out what it was
bout her that drove him nuts. What meant so much. That way,
le could make sure he didn't make the same mistake in the
uture.

"Shawna wanted big," he mused aloud. "Big house, big
noney, big life. She had a craving for fancy stuff. Designer
lothes, exotic vacations, uptown living."

"And your business wouldn't support that?"

"I was still in the army. That was another source of trouble.
was assigned to the Green Berets, she was nagging me to quit.
wanted an overseas post, she wanted big-city luxury." He met
Sierra's eyes, knowing his confusion was clear in his. "She
new what I was all about before we got married."

"Maybe she thought it was what she wanted at the time?"

"Aren't you supposed to trash her or something?" he asked with a strained laugh.

"It sounds like you did fine with that," she said with a laugh. "With both her and yourself. You know, sometimes things just don't work. We want them to, we think we can overcome the obstacles. But the bottom line is sometimes it's just not meant to be."

The tension that had corded Reece's neck since he'd mentioned Shawna started to unknot.

"You're right," he agreed. "We were just too different to make it work. We never stood a chance."

"Oh, no," Sierra corrected before he'd even finished talking. "I didn't say that. My money's on the scenario where you never listened to her, just like you don't listen to me. She probably told you she was scared of your job. Or that she was bored waiting for you to come home all the time. I'll bet she looked for reassurances and you just couldn't hear her."

Reece glared. Self-righteous anger burned in his gut as he leaned forward to make his point.

"What was I supposed to listen to?" he asked in a low, frustrated tone. "She knew what she was getting when she married me. Then she bitched that I was always out playing soldier while she was stuck home playing Susie Homemaker. Whenever I was home, all she did was complain about everything that needed fixing. The dishwasher, the car, our marriage."

After the hot flames of sexual heat had cooled, he'd realized they had nothing in common. But he hadn't been willing to give up. His family didn't divorce. They worked through, they stood by their word. But eventually he'd had to give up. Nothing he'd done was right with Shawna. She'd never been satisfied with what he could offer. With who he was. Reece stared at the water gurgling over the rock and splashing onto the foamy surface below. "Bottom line, she wanted Prada and I couldn't provide."

He heard the rustle of paper, then felt Sierra's hand gently pat the back of his. Not a sexual gesture or even one of pity. It was simple support. Reece turned his hand to slide his fingers into hers and squeezed.

"You know," she told him, her words as soft and sweet as the flower-scented air, "not everyone wants you to solve all their problems for them. Some people might just want you by their side, maybe flexing that gorgeous muscle of yours, while they solve their own problems."

He met her eyes, a mysterious blue in the flickering candlelight. There was sympathy there. But underneath was a strength he'd rarely seen.

It was that strength that scared him.

Reece grabbed her other hand so he could cup both of them between his larger ones. He pulled them close and brushed a kiss over her knuckles. Her eyes flashed sweet and amused, then showed that damned strength again.

He didn't want to scare her. He was glad she was strong. Strong was good. Within limits. But the bottom line was, she had to hear reason.

"But we're not talking about picking out appliances here, sweetheart. We're talking about protecting you from some crazy-ass photo freak who's trying to scare the shit out of you."

"We're also talking about my life," she returned. "If you expect me to trust you to protect it, you have to trust me to actually understand it."

In theory, Reece realized she was right. But the reality was she was simply too close to be objective, too scared to think of all the possibilities. Which was where he came in. To handle those things for her.

But he wasn't about to tell her that.

Instead, he turned one of her hands over and pressed a kiss into her palm. Watching her eyes for another hint of that sweet warmth, he slid his lips in soft butterfly kisses over the tips of her fingers. She gave just the hint of a sigh, and he knew he had to have her.

Reece ran his tongue over the fleshy part of her thumb. Her eyes darkened. He slid her finger into his mouth, just the tip, and sucked. Her breath quickened. He scraped his teeth along the length of her pinky. She wet her lips.

"Have you ever made love outdoors?" he asked in an aroused tone. His favorite turn-on was outdoor sex. There was something so elemental and basic about doing it in nature. That was probably the one most amazing element of his home. Miles and miles of nature, all waiting for sexy times.

"Nature nooky?" she asked. Her smile was slow, wicked and gorgeous. The candlelight glistened off the damp temptation of her bottom lip. Heat, fiery and demanding, speared through Reece's body.

"It's one of my favorite turn-ons," he admitted, trailing his tongue along the side of her hand. "What do you think?"

"Awfully cocky, aren't you?" she said, tapping her finger against his lip.

"Confidence isn't the same as cockiness."

"That's a fine line to walk between the two."

"I've got excellent balance," he reminded her.

"Cocky," she repeated. Her tone was a soft seduction. Teasing, amused and husky.

"I'll show you—"

"Tut tut tut," she tsked, her finger tapping his lip again. "I've seen it, already."

"And yet you doubt my virility?"

"Not what I said," she corrected. "You really don't listen, do you? I said you were cocky to assume we'd make love outdoors."

"Tut tut tut." He offered his own reprimand. "Now who isn't listening? I never said anything about us. I simply asked a question."

She narrowed her eyes.

He waited for the explosion. It wasn't often he cornered her so neatly and he was feeling pretty damned good about it. Definitely worth the temper tantrum about to hit him upside the head.

Once again, though, she surprised him.

"That was a question, wasn't it," she agreed, eyes narrowed in a way that made him wonder if he should move back a few inches. "Have I ever done it outdoors?"

She tilted her head to one side as if in consideration, then gave a slow, single nod of her chin.

Jealousy was an ugly thing. Vicious, biting and nasty in his belly. Reece had to force the muscles in his hand to stay relaxed instead of fisting tight. He didn't want to crush her fragile fingers, and years of training warned him to hide his reaction. Never show weakness, never give the opponent an advantage.

But Sierra saw it anyway.

She pulled her hands from his. Reece frowned. That was it? Yes, she'd already done the sexiest act he could imagine, end of discussion?

Sierra got to her feet and shrugged off her jacket, leaving the delicious skin of her chest and arms bare. He wanted to touch her, to feel the glorious warm silk of her flesh. She carefully laid the jacket over the back of the spare chair, then sat down.

"There was the time in the park," she said, her words shocking him out of his contemplation of the bare skin above the fabric of her tank top.

"A public park?" he blurted out before he could stop himself. He'd never taken her as an exhibitionist. Hell, he loved all the outdoor sex he could get. But the idea of a public park made his willy wilt a little.

"A very public park," she agreed. She gave a deep, satisfied sort of sigh that told him the memory was flipping her switch in a major way. It certainly flipped his. The sound of her sigh combined with the look of pleasure on her face made him rethink public sex. His willy was doing some rethinking too.

Then she smoothed one hand up her arm to her shoulder before trailing her fingers back down so her palm brushed her breast. Reece had to swallow a gulp of soda to wet his suddenly dry throat.

"The park was crowded, because it was one of those perfect spring days. Tender green grass, fluffy white clouds keeping the sun from being too warm. A light breeze—you know, the kind that brushes over your skin like soft fingers?" She waited until he nodded before continuing, "It was beautiful. And I wanted him so bad."

Reece's brow furrowed, but the movement of her hand, the way she was now pausing to cup her breast with each pass, kept him too distracted to work up a good anger. He still managed to fist his hands against his thighs, though.

"He had this intense thing going on, you know? It was driving me crazy. Pretty soon I couldn't resist, and despite the crowds, I grabbed his hand and hauled him off to the thicket of trees behind the entertainment tents."

Her breath shuddered a little as she stopped all pretense of rubbing her arm and cupped both hands over her breasts. Reece reached out to help, but she shook her head.

"We could hear the crowd. Voices, the nearby fountain. Birds in the trees. We didn't care. We tugged at each other's clothes." Her fingers systematically squeezed the soft globes so they rose and fell above the black fabric of her tank top. "He reached under my skirt, and when he realized I wasn't wearing panties, he quit teasing and unzipped his jeans. We did it there, against a tree while the sun shone down on us. I had to bite his shoulder to keep from screaming, the orgasm was so intense."

He groaned at the image. Only instead of some nameless, faceless bastard, it was his shoulder he imagined her biting. His body driving into hers.

"That was the first time," she told him in a low, husky voice. She got to her feet. He pushed back, ready to stand, but she shook her head again. Damn, she was bossy tonight.

Then she tugged her tank top from the waistband of her jeans and pulled it over her head. Against the moonless night, the candle flickered a soft dance of light over her bare torso, gleaming dark against the satin and lace of her bra.

He had to touch her. As if sensing his need, Sierra stepped closer, stopping between his legs. She bent over, her breasts swaying gloriously in their satin cradle. With a soft brush of her lips over his, she pressed his hands down flat against his thighs.

"No touching," she said against his lips. Then, obviously trying to kill him, she flicked the snap of her jeans open and slid the zipper down. She straightened so she stood six inches away, her breasts level with his face, and pushed the snug denim off her hips. He figured it was some female magic created to torture a man that the tight jeans didn't pull the tiny scrap of black satin down with them.

Her pants bunched at her ankles, she stepped back and, after setting the candle on the ground, slid up to sit on the table, then kicked away the fabric.

Reece had just traced his finger over the delicate curve of her calf when she tut-tutted.

"Oh, no you don't," she said. "I'll make you a deal. If you can keep your hands off, I'll tell you more of my outdoor adventures."

His finger froze on her leg. More stories of her and sex?

While she leaned there on the table in front of him, half-naked and looking like the most delicious mouthful of femininity he'd ever tasted?

It sounded like a lesson in torture. And as sick as it was, he didn't want her to stop.

He locked his eyes on hers, leaned forward so his shoulders nudged her thighs apart. His hands now gripping his thighs, he lowered himself until he was pressing his mouth, wet and hot, against the satin covering her sex. He slid his tongue along the edge of the fabric, tasting her musky flavor, teasing her swollen lips.

Sierra mewled in pleasure, then pressed her hands to the top of his head.

"No. No hands, no *mouth*."

"You sure?" he asked, his gaze taking in her dilated pupils, the rapid pulse at the base of her throat and pebbled nipples beneath her satin bra. He dropped his gaze to her now-wet panties.

She squirmed.

"Do you want to hear my adventures?" she asked, obviously willing to leave it up to him. He recalled her accusation that he never listened and wondered if this was some kind of kinky test.

And if he could pass. He had to give it to her, she was doing her best to make it easy for him to want to listen. And making everything else incredibly hard. He shifted, the pressure against his zipper uncomfortably demanding.

Seeing him grimace, she grinned and gestured with her chin. "Tell you what. If you want to touch, you can."

He immediately reached out to slide his finger under the fabric of her panties, flicking the swollen bud already wet with her juices. Before he could press his finger inside her, she grabbed his wrist.

His eyes met hers.

"You can touch," she repeated. "But not me."

It didn't take more than a second to get her meaning. Guilty pleasure filled him, but he didn't hesitate to unzip his jeans and free his straining cock from the tight confinement.

"Tell me," he rasped as he gripped his throbbing flesh in his own hand and started a slow, easy friction with his palm. Her eyes locked on his movements, her breath hitched. She visibly swallowed and took a deep breath as if getting control.

"The next time was in a car."

"What kind of car?"

"You're kidding, right?"

Reece grinned, loving that there could be both sex and banter. That she didn't take it all so seriously, so intensely that the moment couldn't include a little light fun.

"It's a guy thing. Sex in a VW isn't the same as sex in a Corvette."

Her laugh was as baffled as the amused shake of her head. Reece didn't give, though; he just raised his brow.

"I'm not a car aficionado," she protested. His hand stilled. She sighed. "Fine. Let's call it a very powerful, very sexy sports car, okay?"

"Mmm," he approved.

She smirked. Then she took a deep breath and tilted her head back as if gathering the full vision of her memory to share with him.

"So we were in this car. A big, powerful sports car with one of those big motors that made my body shake from the inside out. Like a really good orgasm. But I was so turned on during the drive that each acceleration seemed to vibrate all the way to my damp, aching center."

Hands flat on her legs, she smoothed them up her thighs. Her fingers pressed into the soft flesh, her nails scraping a gentle trail as she slid them upward until she reached her panties, wet from his mouth.

Tilting her head to the side, she held his gaze as if daring him to drop his eyes to her fingers. He could see, just barely out the corner of his eye, that she'd used both hands to cup between her legs.

His hand moved a little faster.

"We reached my house. It was pitch-black outside. All the neighboring houses were dark. My driveway is surrounded by bushes, so nobody could see when I unclipped my seat belt and turned to him." She dropped her eyes to watch Reece stroke himself, her fingers matching his rhythm as she worked her nub still hidden by her panties.

"I had to taste him. I was so turned on I was crazy with need. With desire. I unzipped his pants as he pushed the seat back. It was so dark, I could barely see to take his hard, pulsing dick into my mouth. I sucked and licked his rod. The harder he got, the more turned on I got."

Reece's breath was coming fast now. His hand squeezed and moved in a milking motion as he pleasured himself. He watched through narrowed eyes as she pulled aside her panties, wet with her own juices now.

She didn't touch herself, though. Just let the evening breeze and the heat of his eyes wash over her.

"I sucked until he roared in pleasure. He pulled my mouth away and kissed me at the same time he came," she said softly. Reece's hand spasmed as the memory of himself coming all over her luscious breasts filled his mind.

"Sierra," he muttered in warning. He wasn't going to last much longer. He wanted to touch her, to be inside her when he shot his wad. But if she kept this up, he'd be offering himself up to her flagstone patio instead.

And then to make it worse—or better—she wiggled out of her panties and spread her legs wide so he could see the wet, pink lips beckoning. Still she didn't touch herself. Instead she gripped her thighs, her fingers leaving indentations on the soft flesh as she struggled to keep control.

"The last time," she said, ignoring his warning, "was right here in my backyard. It was like a delicious dessert. The moonless night, the candlelight flickering from the patio as I offered myself to him."

Call him slow, but it wasn't until she mentioned the candlelight that his brain fought its way out of its passion-laced fog of jealousy and realized what she was saying.

"All those times, huh?" he asked, the burning anger he'd tried to ignore subsiding in his gut. "And how were they?"

"They could've been better," she admitted.

Ouch.

Before he could put his ego-shriveling reaction into words, she continued, "They could have been real."

The park. The car. The backyard.

Fantasies, all of them. Fantasies she'd had of him. His ego swelled even bigger than his dick.

Reece grinned, relief and amusement tangling with something deeper. Something more complex and terrifying deep in his gut. Once an obsession, now she was as vital to him as oxygen. He had to have her. Had to keep her. Had to possess her in every way possible.

"I can't do much about the first two," he admitted, getting to his feet. His jeans and boxers dropped and he stepped out of them, taking a second to grab a condom from his pocket. Then he tossed his hat on the grass and in one quick tug had his T-shirt over his head to join the Stetson. "But I can make that last one as real as it gets."

He pulled her onto his lap, spearing her wet folds in a quick, bold move of his hips. Two strokes were all it took to make her body shake. Three and she clenched her thighs on either side of his hips. Five and her pants turned to mewling moans of pleasure.

As soon as he felt her spasming around his dick, he let go. Let the pleasure surge and explode. Stars burned behind his closed eyes as he lost himself in Sierra's body. He was so caught up in the sensations, the power of their lovemaking, that he barely noticed he'd lost his heart to her.

All he knew was that he had, somewhere between the park scene and his orgasm-inspired explosion of stars. And it felt so damned good, he wasn't even going to worry about how he'd recover.

10

"DID YOU GET a facial?" Belle asked as they sat in her office putting the final touches on the next week's events. "You're practically glowing."

"No, although I do have an appointment at The Forsham with Chloe next week for a full treatment," Sierra replied. "Facial, massage, body wrap."

Two weeks of good, down-and-dirty sex and male attention did wonders for a gal's complexion. It also made her a little sore and in need of non-male pampering, she'd discovered. Sierra grinned as she recalled the look on Reece's face when he realized the hot sex she was describing was what she'd imagined doing with him.

"I hate to interrupt whatever put that satisfied smile on your face, but we do have work to do here," Belle said.

Her words, and the slightly irritated tone, snapped Sierra out of her fantasy.

"Sex on the job…" Belle continued with a dramatically disdainful sniff, "even mental sex, is frowned upon while working on the Family events."

"I wasn't thinking about sex," Sierra said defensively. Well, not really. She'd been ruminating over how much damned fun Reece was. In bed, on a table, just to chat with. He kept her on her toes, in every way that counted.

And he seemed to get her like no man ever had. No intimidation, no half-hearted acceptance. Just simple, amused appreciation. Now that he'd taken to heart her demand that he leave her past alone, everything was so close to perfect it almost scared her.

She wasn't ready to share that, though. Not even with Belle. Instead she shrugged and heaved her own exaggerated sigh. "Okay, fine. So I was thinking about sex. But I can wait until I'm back in my office to mentally relive my hot and wild encounters."

Belle smirked. "You're happy."

"You say that in the same tone you'd announce that aliens had landed."

"You're rarely happy." She shook her head before Sierra could voice her protest. "No, you aren't. You are satisfied, content, all those middle-of-the-road things that say you're going in the direction you want. But happy? The giggling, giddy smile-for-no-reason happiness? Rare. Very rare."

"Who wants to walk around smiling for no reason? That's just stupid." Sierra knew she was sidestepping the real meaning of Belle's comment but was not able to help herself. Because her friend was right. Happiness just didn't seem to be her thing.

"You were sitting here smiling for no reason just a minute ago," Belle pointed out.

"Touché." Sierra couldn't stop her grin from flashing again.

"I'm so thrilled for you," Belle said with that giddy about-to-be-married-and-want-the-whole-world-to-be-in-love look that would have freaked Sierra out so much a few months ago. Now it just made her grin. "You and Reece are good together. You'll like happiness."

"It's temporary."

"It doesn't have to be."

"Of course it does." And she was okay with that. As long as she repeated that like a mantra a few million times a day, she was sure by the time he left, she really would be okay with it.

"I'm here, you're here. My life, our business—they are both in L.A."

Who knew happiness hurt so damned much? Sierra ignored the sudden wrench in her gut and shrugged as if it didn't matter.

"We're having fun now. Good times, good sex." She shrugged like that was all she wanted. "And when he finishes this case and heads back home, we'll be done. That's good enough for me."

Belle shot her a look. Sierra rolled her eyes. Yeah, she'd heard for herself how pitiful the lie sounded. But what was she supposed to do? Whine and pout about what she couldn't have? Nag Reece to change and give her the impossible, like his ex-wife had?

"I'll be fine," she said softly. "I'm enjoying the here and now."

And it was a pretty damned good here and now.

"That's good enough," Sierra repeated. She'd make sure of it.

"Maybe—"

"No," Sierra interrupted before her friend could voice any impossible dreams. "What I have is great. I'm satisfied with it."

Belle's face, always so reflective of her emotions, crumpled a little. But she stubbornly forged ahead despite Sierra's warning. "Maybe he'll stick around."

God, she missed the days when Belle backed off easily. Mitch had ruined her passiveness. Sierra sighed and tried not to let the dream take hold in her mind.

"Look, this case is almost done. No—" she ignored Belle's shocked look "—we're no closer to finding the perv. But we're almost through with the Family job. And that's why Reece signed on. To make sure we didn't lose the account. We have the launch event for the magazine, a big tea party, in four days. After that, there's no reason for him to stay."

"He should stay to protect you," Belle snapped, fear and anger clear on her porcelain face.

"I didn't hire him to protect me," Sierra pointed out. She nodded before Belle could speak. "I know you did. But I didn't, okay? I agreed to bring him in so we wouldn't lose this job."

"But that degenerate is getting worse," Belle protested. "That picture was stabbed into your door with a threat. He's moved from sex shots to terrorizing stalker pictures. And he's still sending them to Corinne, even though she doesn't realize it."

"I know." Dread and resignation tangled together in Sierra's gut in a very familiar dance of misery. As usual, she just popped a butterscotch candy and forced herself to suck on it until the urge to run away passed.

Apparently through with orgies, the perv had moved on to pictures of Sierra alone. At the grocery store. Walking to her car. At events or out to dinner with Reece. It was like being followed around by an invisible paparazzi, without the fame and killer paycheck that the leeches used to justify their targets. "But Reece is keeping the pictures from getting to Corinne, so we're not in any danger of losing the account."

"I'm not worried about the damned account," Belle yelled, pushing away from her desk so hard her chair bounced off the wall. She didn't even glance at it. "I'm worried about you. About your safety, first off. And now your heart. Dammit, Sierra, you're finally happy. Truly freaking happy for the first time since I've known you. And you're going to just throw it all away? The safety? The happiness?"

"Don't forget the good sex," Sierra pointed out.

Belle's scream was a work of art. It started low in her throat like a growl and rose to a pitch high enough to break glass. It also brought Cassie, their secretary, running. She hit the doorway gasping. Seeing there was no bloodshed, then catching sight of the anger on her boss's face and the stubborn set of Sierra's chin, she backed away without a word.

"Nice," Sierra said. "If the pervy pictures didn't scare her off, that'd probably do the trick."

"What the hell is wrong with you?" Belle demanded as she stormed around her desk to loom over Sierra like a seriously pissed-off china doll.

"At the moment, possible hearing loss."

The rage flaring in Belle's green eyes warned Sierra that she might have finally gone too far. She sighed. In trying to keep her walls up, to protect herself, she was hurting Belle. That wasn't okay.

"Look, there's no point in getting angry," Sierra said softly. "I love you for caring and wanting to change this. But it is what it is."

"You're just going to sit there on your ass and let your life fall apart?"

Sierra didn't bother pointing out how dramatic and inaccurate that accusation was. She knew Belle was scared by the stalker, and still living in that la-la engagement fog that made her think happy-ever-after was possible for more than the chosen few.

Instead, Sierra leaned forward and took both of Belle's hands in hers. "Sweetie, listen to me. This stalker thing could go on for years. Even the cops admitted that they rarely catch freaks like this. I'm not worried about it, okay?" She was lying, but Belle didn't need to know that. "I'm sure once he sees that he's not achieving whatever his goal is, he'll fixate somewhere else."

Belle's bottom lip trembled, but she didn't say anything.

"Reece can't keep hanging around, okay?" No matter how much she wanted him to. She had no illusions that she would ever get Belle's type of happy-ever-after. She blinked quickly to clear the tears from her eyes, then shrugged. "His life is back in Kentucky. And mine is here. I wouldn't give up what I have here to chase a guy across the country and I wouldn't ask—or let—him do that for me."

"He was offered a job here," Belle blurted out. Her eyes went wide and she pressed her lips together. Obviously that was one of those pillow secrets she wasn't supposed to share.

Sierra's heart raced at the possibility. A tiny spark of hope flared. Then she stamped it out. No. He'd never move to the West Coast. If he were considering it, he'd have said something.

Seeing the devastation in Sierra's eyes, Belle winced and then squeezed her friend's hands. "Even if he doesn't move out here, he's got to finish the job. He's a security specialist. Not an overworked cop. He was hired to find and stop this pervert and I refuse to release him from this job until he does what he was hired for."

"And I refuse to let this draw out to the point where it hurts," Sierra said, swallowing painfully over the lump in her throat. "You have to accept that. I need to know this will end after next weekend, when the Family tea is over. I need that."

She had to have an end date. Something to hold on to that let her feel as if she had some sort of control. She wasn't scared of the stalker. Nasty pictures had nothing on the emotional desert she saw in her mind whenever she imagined life after Reece left.

She'd tried to work through the scenarios, but none offered hope. And she wasn't the kind of gal who held on without hope. Hell, she rarely held on even with guarantees. So an exit date was mandatory.

"What if the stalker situation escalates?" Belle asked quietly.

"What if an earthquake swallows California?" Sierra shot back. "I can't base my decisions on what-ifs. You know that as well as I do."

Belle nodded, then heaved a sigh so big it ruffled Sierra's hair. "Fine. But I'm making you wear a magenta bridesmaid dress. Just so ya know, if we'd had a double wedding, you'd have got out of it."

Shocked amusement broke the tension, making Sierra laugh like crazy. "My only escape from Pepto pink is to get married? Oh please, I'd rather wear the stomach-turning dress down Rodeo Drive than that."

Belle's lips twitched. Fear and worry still lurked in her green eyes, but after a quick squeeze she let go of both Sierra's hands and the issue.

Twenty minutes later, Sierra collapsed in her own office chair. With a sigh, she kicked off her heels, curled her feet under her and laid her head back on the chair cushion. Eyes closed, she visualized all the stress knotted throughout her body being released, pouring away. A few deep yoga breaths and she was calm enough to open her eyes again.

Damn.

She didn't know which was worse. Belle's fear. Or the seed of hope she'd planted when she'd mentioned Reece's job offer. Sierra knew better than to hope. It was a waste of emotion and energy to dream that this fling between her and Reece would be—could be—anything more than a quick flare of sexual heat.

Sure, they'd had a great time together the last couple of weeks. But that was as much due to the fact that they had no expectations of each other beyond the great sex.

But for one second, just after Belle had mentioned the job offer, Sierra had dared to dream. To wonder what it'd be like if Reece were around for a little longer than temporary. To think of what they'd be like down the road. How they'd work things out.

It'd been too sweet a picture to hold for more than a few seconds. Not because it was too fake. But because it was so real it made her hurt.

Her phone rang, pulling her out of her reverie. Drained, Sierra just stared. Then with a sigh, she straightened her shoulders, plastered on her professional smile and grabbed the receiver.

"Sierra Donovan, can I help you?"

"You little bitch."

The room spun once in a slow, dark circle. Bells chimed a dark warning in Sierra's head as she struggled for breath. Her feet dropped to the floor and she automatically felt for her shoes. If she ever needed Manolo-inspired confidence, it was this second.

"Aunt Rose, what a lovely surprise."

"Lovely, is it? Still a disrespectful smart-ass, aren't you?"

"Didn't you always preach living up to one's full potential?" Sierra shot back, her shoes giving her a good dose of bravado. Might as well get in a few kicks early. They'd be squashed as the conversation went on.

"What the hell do you think you're playing at?"

"I'm assuming this is our version of old home week. You know, where you call me at my place of business to insult and degrade me, maybe throw out a few threats and stir up ugly memories?" Pissed that her buttons were so easily pushed, Sierra heard her voice take on an edge. "And I live up to all of your expectations by shooting back smart-ass comments, ignoring your threats and maybe toss out a few memories of my own."

Silence.

Not the comfortable, contemplative kind. But the heavy silence that warned her to find protection. She'd learned in the first month living with her aunt and uncle to gauge the difference. This type of silence had become her three-second warning to find a wall, large piece of furniture or escape route in order to avoid being pelted by flying breakables during one of her aunt's tantrums.

Or in her uncle's case, to simply hide.

He hadn't thrown things. No, he was all about catching things…her in particular.

"You think you're so special, don't you?" her aunt spat out. Sierra caught the hint of a slur in her words and glanced at the clock. Apparently the drinking hour had moved from four o'clock to two.

When she'd first moved in with her relatives, Aunt Rose's drinking had never started earlier than six. Then Uncle Peter had been caught in the pantry with the chef's assistant. The brandy had started making a five o'clock appearance.

By the time Sierra went to college, he'd been caught diddling the cook, the maid and the dog groomer. Aunt Rose had put the Baccarat crystal decanters in each room of the house to good use. It made it easier, Sierra knew, for her to ignore Uncle Peter's sexual proclivities.

"I don't know about special," Sierra said slowly, trying to find a way around the confrontation before it got ugly. "I'm just doing my best to live my life."

"And as usual, your way of living your life ends up bringing your trash and ugliness into mine."

Sierra frowned. "I beg your pardon?"

"How dare you send that…that man here? To my house, to question me. You have the utter nerve to share family business? Business that you know damned well you're to blame for. You and your tight little body, your tiny little shorts and your snotty big attitude."

Sierra had to wait for the panic to subside before she could find the candy in her drawer.

This was bad. She didn't even bother sucking on the peppermint, instead crunching it into pieces as she tried to figure out what to do.

"I didn't send anyone to see you," she offered, although she knew it was futile to protest. Had the cops found some proof that Uncle Peter was behind the pictures? Had they tied him in somehow?

"Are you calling me a liar? We had a deal, young lady. I keep your dirty little secrets and you stay the hell out of my world. And now you, in your fancy-ass uptown world, think you can just break agreements, ruin reputations, cause trouble?" Her aunt's voice rose with each word, until she hit a crystal-shattering shriek. "I think you've forgotten who you're dealing with here."

"No," Sierra said quietly. As much as she tried, she never managed to forget what her aunt and uncle were capable of.

Her aunt's screech rivaled Belle's. Sierra held the phone away and sighed. Twenty-seven was way too young to be fitted for a hearing aid.

"I didn't send anyone to bother you," she repeated.

"What kind of trouble have you started this time?" her aunt demanded.

Anger, built up over weeks of being terrorized with sexually explicit pictures, finally exploded. "I didn't do a damned thing. I'm doing my job. Living my life. I haven't hurt anybody. But does that matter? No. Some sick pervert is stalking me, sending me filthy pictures and now following me around with a camera and making threats."

Silence.

Sierra clenched her jaw to stop it quivering and forced the tears back. When her aunt didn't say anything, her heart hoped for one brief second that maybe, just maybe, they'd found a bridge. That fabled connection between them forged by Sierra's late mother's blood.

Then, "Leave it to you to create a scene." There was a clink of glass against glass—refill time, Sierra figured. "I've never seen a person more gifted at stirring up conflict and drama than you are. Just like your mother, of course. She could create a fake stalker from a Dear Occupant letter. Self-aggrandizing attention seeking is all it is."

"Why don't I send you some of these fake pictures just for a few dramatic thrills?" Sierra snapped, as always incensed beyond watching her mouth when Rose started tossing insults at her mother. "The blood-covered ones are especially self-aggrandizing. In a stomach-turning way, of course. But hey, what do you care about a little blood and pain? As long as it doesn't leave a mess on your Aubusson carpet, it's no skin off your ass."

Even as the words spewed out of Sierra's mouth, she cringed and wished she could take them back.

"And this is why that…man—that cowboy—came to my house? To accuse me of this sordid act?"

Cowboy? It hadn't been a cop doing his job. Nobody following a tip. Instead it was Reece. Poking his nose in, ignoring her wish that he stay the hell out of her past. It was all Sierra could do not to scream in fury.

"Or maybe he was here to accuse your uncle?" Rose continued coldly. "Are you trying to play those same old games again, miss? Didn't you learn anything last time?"

Sierra closed her eyes. Late at night, when she couldn't quite control her thoughts, she'd wondered if her uncle might be behind the pictures. The tackiness of them, the sexual perversions, they were all right up his deviated alley. But she knew better. She wouldn't put those pictures past him, of course. But if it'd been him, they'd have come with a price tag. A demand for money. Had he shifted to a nonprofit form of torment? Or, given her continued business success, was she working up to a big payoff?

"Perhaps my attorney should remind you of the penalty of slander?" Rose threatened. "You remember him, don't you? I'd have thought the defamation lecture would stick with you a little longer, miss. But it sounds like we need a refresher course."

"I told you, I didn't know anything about the visit. I'm

sorry, though, that someone bothered you." She felt sick at the flood of memories of all the other times Rose had sidestepped responsibility or reassigned blame to Sierra. Before her aunt could attack again, Sierra played the trump card. "But if someone caused you distress, I'll make it up to you."

The silent reaction to her offer was marred by the sick churning of nausea in her stomach.

Sierra knew she was giving in. She knew her aunt had no leg to stand on, no real threat to hold over her except exposure. But the fact was, they had made a deal. Her relatives hadn't fought her emancipation declaration. In return, she'd stupidly signed a non-slander agreement with their attorney that mandated that she couldn't mention their names, belittle their care or give any hint that her relatives had been anything but circumspect in taking her in. An agreement that she now knew wasn't legally binding, given the coercion and her age.

But still, a promise was a promise. She'd agreed to stay out of their lives and keep quiet about her uncle's wandering hands and perverted mouth. As long as she left them alone, she could keep her past behind the locked door the way she needed to. Because as much as she liked to pretend she didn't care what people thought, she knew she couldn't stand the idea of her relatives' version of the truth getting out—that she'd been a teenage slut hell-bent on seducing an older man and then attempting to murder him.

But now Reece, ignoring her request to stay the hell out of her past, had broken her part of the deal. Granted, it was more than ten years since they'd made it. But her word didn't have an expiration date. Nor did her relatives' expectations.

Then her aunt said in a triumphant, satisfied tone, "I'd like a vacation. Somewhere warm and tropical."

"Just you?"

"Your uncle is…away."

Away where? Away creating disgusting pictures? Sierra's fear that he was behind the stalking intensified. After all, even if she knew he was, her aunt wouldn't bat an eyelash at denying it. She'd post the envelopes herself and still straight out tell Sierra she was imagining it all.

Sucking in a deep breath, Sierra tried to get a hold of herself. She needed to quit freaking out. Peter was probably just off with another bimbo somewhere. Sierra wanted to feel sorry for her aunt. To pity the woman for the treatment she endured. Except Rose chose to be there. Just like she'd chosen to believe her husband's protest that Sierra had come on to him, that she'd teased and tormented him until he couldn't stand it anymore and had to touch her.

Sierra popped another peppermint into her mouth, sucking on the sugary treat this time instead of decimating it as she and her aunt made the trip arrangements.

But the sweetness of the candy was ruined by the bitter taste of salt as tears trickled down her face.

REECE SHOOK Toby's hand and followed him through the photography studio. "I appreciate the tour," he told the quiet assistant.

The diminutive guy just shrugged. Reece wondered if he'd ever learned the art of conversation or if it was some creative foil to build mystery. He glanced at the guy in the baggy, food-stained T-shirt and unremarkable chinos and figured it was the former rather than the latter.

"Other than Sears for family holiday shots, I've never seen a photography studio before," Reece commented. He didn't have to fake his interest as he looked around.

The front of the building was all windows, he supposed to catch natural light. For additional lighting there were tall lamps with umbrella attachments tucked aside in a corner and a wall with what looked like huge rolls of fabric on the ceiling. The floor was concrete, but Reece could see a variety of coverings stacked behind the lamps.

"Tristan actually takes his pictures here?" he asked. "Doesn't he worry about an unwelcome audience with those windows?"

Toby shrugged. "He does the nudes somewhere else."

Literally or figuratively? Reece pulled a face. Recalling Mitch's teasing words at the gallery showing, he had to force himself not to ask Toby if he considered assisting on those shoots a job perk. The guy didn't seem to have much of a sense of humor.

"So is this it?" Reece asked, waving his hand around the studio. He'd conned his way into this tour when he'd chatted with Tristan two weeks ago at Eventfully Yours. The day of his first date with Sierra, as a matter of fact. He'd had to time it right, though. He'd listened to the girls' plans, then gauged when the photographer would be away. Because Toby had been there when Tristan had issued the invitation, Reece had just acted like he'd mixed up the times today and the assistant had reluctantly agreed to give him the tour without his boss.

The advantage of Tristan being gone was double. He could snoop to his heart's content, since he didn't figure the kid would catch on. And this way nobody was going to tell Sierra he was here.

Crucial point, since she'd been adamant that her friend was completely innocent. But Reece was starting to think she was mistaken. Loyalty was a good thing, but not when it was used against you.

And he was sure that was the case. He'd ruled out her uncle. And while his instincts screamed that Tristan was just too obvious, sometimes people were stupid enough to think the obvious would be ignored.

Reece wasn't stupid. And he didn't ignore anything.

"So you're a photographer, too?" he asked randomly. He

didn't care, he just wanted an excuse to poke for clues. He figured the longer he kept the guy talking, the more he'd be able to see.

"Someday," the guy muttered, his tone so low Reece could barely make out the words. "Tristan is training me. He's like a mentor, you know? I work here cheap, he gives me tips and stuff."

"Sounds like a deal."

An odd look flickered in Toby's dull brown eyes. It was gone too fast for Reece to decipher, but it made the hair on the back of his neck prickle. A trick of the light, maybe? He mentally flipped through his research. Despite Mitch's jokes and Toby's act at the exhibit, the kid was gay. That, combined with the female-obsessed psychological profile Reece had run on the perp, had knocked him off the suspect list. Besides, the kid had been right there in full sight at the gallery when the perv had been taking pictures. Airtight alibi.

Toby flashed a shy sort of grin and said, "Yeah. It's a pretty good deal. I tried to break in on my own, but this business is a killer. It's all about contacts, you know? About connections and that networking crap. Not much respect for art in L.A. Not when there's so much competition."

"Tristan seems to have done okay for himself," Reece said with a friendly smile of his own, grabbing the opening. "I mean, he's got gallery shows happening, contracts with biggies like Eventfully Yours. That's pretty solid for a town like this, isn't it?"

"He knows how to work it."

I'll just bet he does, Reece thought as he stepped through the studio to what was apparently an in-house exhibit.

The small room was covered in cork, pictures tacked up on every surface. Naked women, stunning scenery, random products like coffee filters. Color, black-and-white, sepia-toned. It was like a teenage girl's poster-covered wall.

"Wow."

Toby smirked and gave a little shake of his head. "It's a

mess. I keep telling him he needs to give this up, put the key shots on a disk and turn this room into something that makes sense."

Disk, huh?

"Photography is mostly digital these days, isn't it?" Reece asked as if he hadn't a clue. When Toby nodded, he continued, "I'd think it'd be a lot easier to, what'd you call it? Make a disk? Yeah, that would be a lot easier than printing them all out like this."

"Right. You get it. Tris, though, he's weird about it. I think it's because he's old. Old and old school, you know? He learned to shoot back when they developed film. He says he needs prints." The younger man's shyness was fading as he warmed to the subject. He stabbed a finger at one of the pictures, a nude shot in a garden. "He says he needs to see it on paper to judge its worth. Crazy, if you ask me. Waste of time and energy. Money, too."

Reece knew from his data search that he was a good four years older than the photographer. Which in Toby's estimation probably made him older than dirt.

"He's good at computer stuff?" Reece fished.

"Nah. He sucks at it. I figured I could take classes, learn it, then show him, ya know?"

"Good thing he's got you looking out for him, hmm?" Reece said, wanting to hear more about the digital angle. Better yet, he wanted to wrangle an invitation to see the computer.

"He'd be nowhere without me," came the quiet reply. The kid settled back into his sulky persona so fast, Reece wondered if he'd imagined the animation.

"I had no idea pictures had gotten so techno," Reece said, returning to the topic at hand. "I guess you all have to know computers pretty well these days."

"I may not know the ins and outs of digital editing, but I know how to use a computer," Toby said with a shrug. Reece, who actually remembered a time in his life without a PC, suddenly felt as old as this kid probably thought him. "We've got a sweet system."

"Yeah? How does it tie in with the picture business?"

Toby launched into a detailed and enthusiastic description of his job and how he'd customized different programs to meet their needs. As he talked, he led Reece through a hallway with what looked like dressing rooms, some with full mirrors surrounded by lights—the kind Reece had only seen before in movies.

They came to another room, this one as big as the front studio. One wall was covered with a locked glass case. Behind the glass, Reece noted, were a variety of cameras. Two huge desks sat in the middle of the room with a light board and long waist-high table at the other end.

It was pure masculine clutter. Magazines were strewn everywhere. Books, earmarked and worn, were piled high on a chair in the corner. And right there, center stage, was a shelf filled with large how-to books. Smack in the middle of *How to Set a Perfect Table* and *Monster Makeup Made Easy* was *Photo Editing for Idiots*.

Bingo.

"Does Tristan ever take on outside work? You know, editing pictures he didn't take, maybe?" Thinking fast, Reece lied, "My parents' anniversary is coming up and they don't have a decent picture from their wedding. They do have a bunch of shots but all of them are missing one or two people. Could he put them together into a single picture? You know, edit it or something?"

Toby smiled eagerly. "Sure. He does it all by hand, so it's pricier than most guys. I've got his editing portfolio right here. You want to take it? Look it over and see if it's the kind of work you want done? You're in tight with Sierra, so I know he won't mind."

Well, that was easy. Too easy?

"Sure," Reece said, watching as the young man unlocked a file cabinet and pulled out a leather case, flat and about a foot and a half by two feet.

Perfect. He'd found a fragment of a thumbprint on the last photo. Not enough to run, but enough that if any of the papers Tristan had touched in this file had a match, he would have cause to bring the cops in.

He didn't know what would thrill Sierra more: his tying this case up so quickly, or his plans to invite her to Kentucky.

He couldn't wait to find out, though.

He hoped it was a good enough reaction to balance the fury she'd have over his busting her friend.

11

"YOU'RE FIRED."

Barely glancing at her, Reece held up one hand to silence her and kept talking on the phone.

"Hang on," he mouthed.

And he went right back to ignoring her.

Fury blurring her vision, Sierra swung her purse off her shoulder and heaved it across the room. She cussed a blue streak when it sailed past his head and thumped just short of the wall behind him.

But it got his attention. He gave her a shocked frown. Then he glanced behind him at the black leather missile.

"I'll call you back," he said, then pushed the phone's Off button.

He glanced at the purse again and offered her a taunting smile. "Sweetheart, you need to announce yourself a little better. I almost didn't hear you over the slamming door and cussing in my reception area."

Sierra glared, anger making spots flash in front of her eyes. "Do you think you're funny?"

He lowered his laptop cover and planted one elbow on his desk, then tugged at his bottom lip as if he were trying to hide his smile.

"No?" he answered, apparently thinking he was some kind of cute. She wished she hadn't thrown her purse at him like that.

If she still had it, she was now in a much better position to hit him and wipe that smirk off his face.

"I told you to leave it alone," she snarled, her words rising with each breath. "Where do you get off? What gives you the right? How freaking dare you?"

There. That swiped the smirk right off his damned face. With a frown, Reece stood and placed both hands on his desk. Leveling the playing ground, she knew. As if she could be intimidated by a guy she'd eaten chocolate lava cake off.

"Maybe you'd like to clarify your rant a little?" he invited.

"Maybe you'd like to get screwed."

"Offering?"

"Never again."

"Now that hurts."

"Not nearly as much as I'd like to hurt you," she promised. Sierra stormed forward and slammed her fists to her hips. "I told you, dammit. I warned you to leave my life alone. Not to stir up shit. Why the hell didn't you listen to me?"

Furious that her voice cracked, she tried to force back the tears. God, even now, he wouldn't take her seriously. As if it were all a joke.

At her words, though, the teasing cowboy disappeared and soldier boy took his place. Sierra warned herself to quit getting turned on by the sight. Reece's jaw hardened. His eyes turned to stone, not a pretty sapphire but hard granite. And his shoulders, so graspable during sex, went military-rigid.

"It's my job to offer security. It's also my job to investigate any possible suspects who might be behind the threat."

"No. It was your job to pacify my client. To step in, play bodyguard and assure her that this picture crap wasn't going to affect the work Eventfully Yours had been contracted to do."

"That's not what I agreed to when you hired me."

"I didn't freaking hire you," she snapped back. Frustration and fury were a potent cocktail, sending her head spinning and her emotions swirling out of control. "You offered, Belle accepted."

"Regardless," he said, once again ignoring her. Sierra would have screamed if her ears weren't already ringing. Instead she growled low in her throat and imagined how he'd like it if she bounced his laptop off his pointed head.

"I had a job to do," Reece explained in a calm, patient tone. As if she were a four-year-old needing a nap. "It isn't playacting for me. I take my work very seriously. If you saw it as anything else, that's your problem."

"You've definitely made it my problem now, haven't you?"

"No. I've worked to make you safe. There's a difference."

"Safe how? By stirring up problems? By throwing around unfounded accusations and making people pissed off at me? I had less stress with the pervert than I do now, thanks to you."

Reece threw his hands up in frustration, obviously done trying to pacify her. Sierra gave a vicious little grin, glad she could actually push his buttons.

"Look, you don't like the way I work, fine. But I'm not apologizing for checking out metro boy. He's always been a prime suspect because of both proximity and profession. I'm even more suspicious after visiting his studio."

Sierra barely heard a word after metro boy. Buzzing filled her head, fury flicking like angry bumblebees in front of her eyes.

"I can't believe you." She didn't even raise her voice. Instead, she offered her shock in a low, dull tone. Because as far as she was concerned, she no longer felt any emotion for Reece. "I told you it couldn't be Tristan. If you cost me the best photographer in L.A. because you're a gung-ho idiot, I'm going to do you permanent damage."

"Just because you dated the guy doesn't mean it's not him. If anything, that increases the likelihood that it is."

"Tristan is my friend." She ground out the words.

"Friend or not, he's a photographer. He's losing money through his contract with you. And for all you know, he's got the hots for your body. Then you emasculated him by shoving him in the friend category and ruined his chances to get you into bed."

"Not everyone thinks with their dick," she informed him with a haughty sneer.

"You only say that because you don't have one, sweetheart."

"You won't have one, either, if you don't back off."

Unfazed by her threat, Reece leaned back on his desk and crossed his arms over his chest. "What makes you so sure metro boy isn't your stalker?"

Her anger stopped its breakneck race to implosion. She eyed him mistrustfully, but saw no trace of mockery or condescension on his face.

"These pictures are computer-altered," she reminded him. "Tristan is so anti-computer that he doesn't even have an e-mail account."

"The two of you play video games," he argued. "He has a Web site."

"The games were my attempt to help him overcome his technophobia. Toby handles his Web site. If you check it, though, there is no e-mail address. He doesn't trust it so he insists that anyone wanting to contact him do it by phone."

His eyes turned cautious. Frowning, he shoved his fingers into the front pocket of his jeans and considered her gravely.

"From your reaction, I'm guessing you didn't realize I'd been to DeLaSandro's studio? Maybe you could clarify what you're pissed about, then."

"Why? So you can make sure you don't confess any other crimes against my privacy?"

"Doing my job isn't a crime." His irritation at having to defend himself was clear.

"You had no right to dig into my past and drag it into my present." Clamping her lips shut to keep from spilling how badly he'd hurt her by stirring up her past, she waved a hand at him. "You overstepped your bounds and went way outside your job description."

"Outside my bounds?" His words were low, bitten off as if he couldn't stand the taste of them.

He straightened and stormed forward so fast she gasped. Sierra steeled herself, but he just brushed past her. With a clanging that made her press two fingers to her temple and wish for a painkiller, he yanked open a file cabinet drawer.

He turned back around with a folder clenched in his fist. Aiming it at her like a weapon, he said, "This is the kind of shit that's been coming in, sweetheart. This is the threat you're dealing with. You want to call this a prank, a pain in the ass? You go right ahead."

Refusing to let him see how much he was scaring her, Sierra snatched the folder from his hand. She flipped it open, and immediately wished she hadn't. Stomach pitching dangerously, she sucked in shallow breaths through her teeth.

"Why haven't I seen these?" she asked faintly.

"What's the point? Would they help you get through the day-to-day? Why do you think you've been so busy lately? Belle's making sure you're never alone." Reece snatched the folder and grabbed random pictures, holding them in front of her for emphasis. "Last week this bastard followed you to the grocery store. Before that, the dry cleaner's. Here's one of you driving. He was right freaking next to you."

She was glad he'd taken the folder from her. Her hands were shaking so badly she'd have dropped it.

She'd thought Reece was spending his every waking minute with her out of lust and maybe, just maybe, some burgeoning emotional connection. But he'd been protecting her.

She knew she should be grateful. She would be grateful. Just as soon as she patched together the missing pieces of her heart.

"What do you want?" Reece demanded, oblivious to her turmoil. "Do you want this creep caught? Do you want him stopped? To find out what kind of sick mind is behind these disgusting pictures? Or do you want to bury your head in the sand and pretend this is just going to fade away? Because it's not, sweetheart. It's ugly, it's real and it's not going anywhere."

Sierra wanted to blow him off. To tell him just how unimpressed she was with his exaggerations and melodrama. Except images of the recent pictures, the ones he'd hidden from her, were burned in vicious detail on her brain.

The threats. The ugliness. The degradation. They all pounded on her nerves, mocking her little-girl fears. She'd spent fourteen years hiding from her uncle. What if her suspicion was right and he was behind this?

"You visited my aunt and uncle," she blurted out.

Reece narrowed his eyes and nodded.

"You infuriated my aunt. She's livid that I'd bring the taint of this kind of drama anywhere near them."

"And she seemed so nurturing and concerned," he mused sarcastically.

"Oh, believe me, she's concerned. She's concerned with what the neighbors will think. She's all for nurturing her reputation and status, no matter how difficult certain nasty little perversions make it for her."

Reece's narrow-eyed look made her review her words. Sierra bit her lip, realizing how much she might have given away. Maybe he hadn't clued in?

"Nasty little perversions in general? Or are we talking about someone's in particular?"

Sierra gave a jerky shrug.

"I didn't get to meet your uncle," he mused, his eyes glued

on her face. Sierra fought to keep a neutral expression. "Maybe he'd have had a little more insight for me?"

"He wouldn't have told you any more than whatever you got out of Rose," she said. "Less, probably. I'm sure she happily filled you in on what a nightmare I was for them? How ungrateful and disrespectful it was of me to land on their doorstep and ruin their lives?"

He didn't have to say anything. She saw the affirmation on his face. Sierra felt nothing. No sadness. No regret and, oddly enough, not even embarrassment at his having an ugly peek into her past.

Hell, he'd been looking at pictures of her having sex with barnyard animals for the last month. Why should her family be any more humiliating?

As long as the dirty little details didn't come out, that was.

"Are you saying I should dig deeper into your relatives?"

Horror filled her eyes. "God, no. Didn't you listen when I walked in here? You're fired. I want you to drop the whole thing. Leave my friends alone. Stay out of my past. Just let it go."

"Didn't you look?" he paraphrased, grabbing the folder of pictures off his desk and shaking it at her. "I'm not letting some sicko get away with this."

"It's not up to you," she insisted fervently. She knew she sounded desperate but couldn't help it. She was frantic. It was all she could do not to beat on his chest and scream at him. He had to do as she asked. To step away and leave it alone before things got really ugly. "Don't you ever listen?"

"I don't walk away from a job unfinished," he insisted flatly. "If you want to stick your head in the sand and ignore reality, that's your choice. But I won't. I'll find the stalker. I'm not stopping until I do. If DeLaSandro's behind this, I'll find out. If it's someone else, someone from your past, I'll find that out, too. But I won't leave you in danger. I won't let the stalker win."

Pressure pounded inside her skull. She couldn't stand it. Frustration and pain twined together, snapping the last thread of her control. Unable to do otherwise, she lashed out.

"What the hell is your problem? Are you so jealous of Tristan you can't look past the obvious? Or is it pure pigheaded cowboy stubbornness that makes you refuse to consider that someone might have the right to say no to playing your little game?"

REECE CLENCHED his jaw so tight his teeth hurt. Damned if he knew what Sierra's problem was. She'd stormed in here all het up over her bitchy aunt calling her and tried to fire him. He'd showed her proof positive why that was a stupid idea, but did she back down?

Hell, no. She just got more stubborn and unreasonable. Anger flamed in her blue eyes, and her hair was practically electric with the force of her temper. He watched her chest heave, the deep breaths pulling her silky shirt tighter to her breasts with each inhalation.

Only a pig would get turned on at the sight of a woman ready to chop him off at the balls. Reece swept his gaze back up to meet Sierra's, noting the high color on her cheeks. She was the most alive, the most passionate woman he'd ever met.

He might as well have *oink* tattooed to his forehead.

Until she opened her mouth.

"Now I can see why your ex tossed your ass out," she spat.

Reece glared. Since when was his past up for discussion?

"She didn't toss. I walked. Just like I'll be walking when I'm done here."

Sierra's eye roll was a work of art. It mocked his words, his intentions and his manhood all with a flick of her lashes.

"I should have known," he mused in disgust. "Shawna wanted Prada and she didn't care what she did to get it. You *are* Prada and you got it yourself. But underneath the fancy label, you're both exactly the same."

The look she gave him was a mixture of pity and annoyance. "You're totally oblivious, aren't you? Your ex wanted a little proof that you gave a damn. But you never listened enough to catch a clue."

Ignoring his growl, she strode around him to pick up her bag.

"And by the way," she said as she swung her purse over her shoulder, turned and headed for the door, swinging her hips in pure sass, "you're not walking out. I am."

"You can't always run," he said, not sure where the words came from. Or why he even bothered.

He wanted to force her to stay. He wanted to grab her, to hold her close and keep her safe. But he knew Sierra. She had to make it all right in her own head.

At the door, she stopped and took a shuddering breath. He could see her shoulders shake with it. Concern doused his fury.

"My uncle keeps a house, properties, under the name Peter Sullivan. If he's doing anything dirty, that's where you'd find it." The fear was so intense in her voice, it practically dripped on the carpet. Just as strong, though, was the pain. He couldn't stand it. He stepped forward.

"Sierra—"

"No," she said. She didn't look back, but her shoulders stiffened as if someone had shot steel into them. "We're through. If you have a superhero complex and insist on finishing this job, apparently I have no say. Even though it's my life, you won't listen. But stay the hell away from me."

"WHO THE HELL does she think she is?" Reece demanded two hours later as he wrenched open Mitch's refrigerator to grab his fourth beer. "She figures she's sexy, smart and successful, so that gives her the right to fire me?"

"Nah. She probably figured she'd hired you and that gave her the right to fire you."

"As she so loudly pointed out, she didn't hire me. Belle did." Reece slouched on the couch and took a drink of the beer he didn't even want. But it dulled the pain. He'd never had a woman cause him real pain before, so he didn't know how long the beer would work. Probably not as long as this conversation, from the look in Mitch's eyes.

"What're you gonna do?" Mitch asked in his usual direct way.

Reece gave an angry jerk of his shoulder. What the hell was he supposed to do? Sierra had jumped all over him for doing his job. Thrown a fit because he'd rightfully investigated a suspect. Which was why he'd already run a check on her uncle. And if she'd bothered to trust him with that information a month ago, he'd have had the goods on her uncle's second identity.

The old guy was ass-deep in porn, hookers and kink. And from the looks of his bank accounts, whenever he ran a little dry on the funds to keep himself in the nasty goods, he tapped his niece for a little cash. No wonder her account wasn't flush.

Reece glared at the floor, the beer souring in his stomach. She paid the son of a bitch. Not often. Every few years, a couple grand here and there.

He stared down the long neck of his beer as if he could see the liquid through the dark brown glass.

She'd been abused. He didn't know the extent of it. Bitterness coated his tongue since he couldn't dig for details. She didn't want him involved, hadn't wanted to share. Simply put, it all came down to trust.

She didn't trust him to protect her.

She didn't trust him with her past.

She'd never trust him with her heart.

Reece wanted to throw the bottle across the room. He

wanted to jump up and howl like a wounded animal. To beat the living hell out of the people who'd harmed Sierra.

He wanted to find her, gather her close and promise that nobody would ever hurt her again.

And he knew damned well if he tried to get near her right now, she'd scratch his eyes out. Which was why he'd brought in one of his security team to keep an eye on her. The fact that he had to trust someone else with her safety grated at his ego and nurtured a tiny seed of fear in his gut.

"So what're you going to do?" Mitch asked from across the room. Reece met his cousin's eyes, seeing the question was much bigger than a simple next-step decision.

"I don't know," he admitted.

"I don't think I've ever heard those words out of your mouth before," Mitch said with a humorless little laugh.

Reece grimaced. Then he gathered his beer-soaked thoughts for examination.

"She told me to jump off the case," he stated first. Used to his way of sorting information, Mitch just nodded but didn't say anything. "She's hiding information. She's pissed beyond words."

"Maybe she thinks she has a good reason," Mitch said quietly. Reece glared at his favorite cousin. Then with a grimace, he shifted his gaze to his boots.

The last thing Reece wanted to hear was that Sierra might be right. He was already miserable enough knowing they were through. Throw in his worry over her being vulnerable since she thought he was fired, and that was all he could handle. No way did he want to shoulder any blame to go with his misery and worry.

"I'm not saying she's right—or at least, not completely," Mitch said in the same soothing tone Reece used with skittish horses. "I said that women see things differently than men do."

"You mean they see things wrong."

Mitch smirked. "Cuz, just because she's not on the same page you are doesn't make her wrong."

"She thinks I should have left things alone. Just stood around waiting for someone to attack her instead of going after whoever is behind the threats."

"Then she doesn't know you very well."

Reece considered the idea. Did she know him? She knew what turned him on, that was pure fact. She knew what made him laugh, how to get him out of a bad mood. She knew how important it was for him to do a good job. How much he prided himself on giving his all.

What else was there to know?

How to placate him? How to dance around a topic until he gave up in frustration? How to stroke his ego in order to manipulate the situation?

Reece slid down further on the couch, his beer cradled on his flat belly, and contemplated those choices.

Sierra was one smart gal. If she'd wanted to manipulate him, she was clever enough to figure out how. But she didn't play those kinds of games.

"If I know Sierra," Mitch said quietly, poking at the raw edges of Reece's nerves, "all she wanted was to be in the loop. To know you were including her, not placating her."

Well, hell. Reece closed his eyes and sighed. He'd done everything but pat her on the head and tell her to get him a beer and his slippers.

She'd stepped up to the table and played an honest hand. And she'd expected the same from her partner. Or her opponent. And Reece had been both. And he'd done neither.

Instead he'd done exactly what she'd accused him of doing. Oh, he'd listened. She was wrong there. But he'd gone his own way. Done his own thing and it'd hurt her. Instead of bringing her in, explaining his reasons or even sharing ideas, he'd just forged ahead. At her expense.

Just like he'd refused to take a plum job and move to L.A. Nope, he'd planned on asking Sierra to join him in Kentucky. Figured she could pick up a few catering jobs, maybe start a new business there if she wanted. To hell with the fact that she had a fabulous career here.

He'd only been thinking of himself. Of his wants, his needs. Just like she'd said. But he'd justified it nicely, wrapping it all around his logical reasoning. That way, when she told him where to get off with his offer, he could blame her.

The question was, what was he going to do now? Prove her right? Or prove her wrong?

It wasn't even a choice. The real question was, how was he going to do it?

12

REECE WALKED into DeLaSandro Studios for the second time in as many days, this time glad to see the owner in residence. On the phone, with Toby nowhere to be found, Tristan barely acknowledged Reece's presence. Instead he paced the room, squinting through a camera lens with a phone to his ear.

Intrigued, Reece leaned his shoulder against the doorjamb and waited. As he listened to the photographer talk a mile a minute, he wondered where the camera was that went with the lens.

"Sunrise. I need the filtered light. No, no blondes. They'd fade against the sand. Hmm, no, she's got the style for it, but I'd rather have a redhead. Get Kimmi for styling. Ethereal, gossamer, think butterflies and ballet."

Totally baffled by the conversation, Reece glanced around the large room. Nothing had changed since he'd been here the day before. The computer sat, black screen, in the corner with fabric piled on the keyboard. Classical music, some symphony or other, played tinnily from another room.

"You here for a picture?"

It took Reece a couple seconds to realize Tristan was off the phone and addressing him. "Nah, I'm camera shy."

The guy's expression didn't change. He just stared. Narrow-eyed, contemplative, a little vague. It was like being sized up for a shot. Or having his soul assessed.

Reece shook off the weird feeling and stepped forward, hand out. Tristan didn't hesitate, grasping it in a firm shake.

"Got a minute?" Reece asked him.

Another stare. Then Tristan shrugged and turned toward the back room where the music was playing. "If you talk while I work, sure."

Reece followed him back into what looked like the scene of a department store explosion. Clothes, hats, lingerie. Furniture, appliances, sports equipment.

"Props," Tristan said, seeing the confusion on Reece's face.

The guy was a puzzle. Metro, right down to his silver jewelry, manicured nails and perfectly styled hair. One of those dreamy artists, if the phone conversation Reece had walked in on was anything to go by. Yet he had a grip that guaranteed he'd hold his own in a fight.

Reece had come in to ask Tristan a few questions, to play the expert opinion card and get some advice. His mind warned him to play his cards carefully. But his gut told him to trust Sierra. Since this was advice his gut had never offered before, he was hesitant.

Then he realized he had no choice. Not if he wanted Sierra.

He frowned at Tristan.

"Some pervert is stalking Sierra. He's following her around, taking her picture. He's sending photos and ugly threats, but no demands. Just a lot of head games."

Tristan smirked. "So you knocked me off the short list, huh?"

Reece's lips twitched, but he just shrugged. "You're not surprised about the stalker?"

"I knew there was crap going on. The girls don't bring in security for the uptight and upright." The sneer in his tone made it clear he wasn't impressed by the client.

"You have an issue with Family?"

"Nope. They paid for my new lens."

"Then what's the problem there?"

"They micromanage. Makes me claustrophobic."

And that was it. Instead of expanding on his innocence, Tristan went back to digging through a dresser drawer filled with costume jewelry.

He couldn't be that unaffected, could he?

"Does it bother you that you might be a suspect?" Reece asked.

"What's the point? If I was a suspect, I doubt you'd be taking the chitchat route." Apparently finding what he was looking for, Tristan tossed a fistful of white beads into a bag, then added a few strands of glitter. "If you hadn't made up your mind, you'd be trying the intimidation tact. That or still investigating behind the scenes."

Right. Maybe those eyes did look right through to the soul?

"The stalker's pictures are all computer-enhanced—cropped images, poorly pasted scenes," Reece told him. "Sierra says you're not into computers. From what I've seen, she's right."

Tristan shot him a long, level look. His pitch-black gaze didn't show a single emotion. Then he shrugged. "I'd be an idiot to tell her otherwise, wouldn't I?"

"You would," Reece agreed with an easy grin. He tilted his Stetson back on his forehead and nodded. "And you don't strike me as an idiot."

"You don't strike me as careless," Tristan returned, his expression unchanged. Reece was glad he wasn't playing poker with the guy. He gave nothing away. "So you must have more to clear me than Sierra's opinion of my photo-editing skills."

Considering those words and the challenge that came with them, Reece rocked back on his heels. He wasn't a guy who put a lot of stock in intuition. He believed in facts. Proof, one way or the other.

The decision loomed in front of him. He had no leg to stand on, nothing to back him up. And his reasons were all the wrong ones. Except that they weren't.

"Sierra trusts you implicitly. She is positive you're clean."

For the first time since Reece had walked in, emotion flickered on the photographer's face. "You're letting me off the hook because you don't want to piss off your girlfriend?"

Smirking as he thought of the look on Sierra's face if she heard herself called anyone's girlfriend, Reece shrugged. "Nah. I piss her off all the time. But I have to ask myself this. A guy is stalking her for a reason. It's not just random cheap thrills. He wants something."

"To mess with Sierra's head?"

Reece frowned. "Why do you say that?"

"She's edgy, closed in lately. I haven't seen her like that since school. She ever tell you why we're so tight?"

Reece hated to admit she'd refused to share that information, so he just shrugged.

"She needed a loan to support herself after she got cut off from her asshole relatives. I had money, she had something I wanted." The photographer leaned back, shooting Reece an assessing look.

"You helped her out?" he clarified, not rising to the bait. Sierra said there hadn't been anything between them. He believed her.

"She helped *me* out," Tristan said with a shrug before admitting, "I'm dyslexic. That's why I don't do the computer thing, probably why she was so sure I wasn't behind the pictures. She helped me study, find ways to deal with it. In return, I loaned her money. Wanted to give it to her, but you might have noticed she can be a little stubborn."

"Her family didn't support her," Reece clarified.

Tristan shook his head.

"Hardly. She came into a small trust when she turned eighteen. Enough to get her through college."

Reece experienced a wave of disgust. Not in anger at her relatives, although he had plenty of that churning through his system. No, this disgust was directed at himself. He'd judged her. Compared her to his scheming, label-obsessed ex. Sierra couldn't be more different than Shawna. He'd seen it himself. Sierra was careful with money—his investigation had proved she lived on a budget. And sure, she dressed high-end, but he'd come to realize that rather than a closet full of pricey clothes, she had a few designer pieces and a lot of staples. God, he was a stupid son of a bitch.

"And now someone's trying to jeopardize everything she's built," Reece mused quietly.

"You gonna stop them?"

"I plan to."

"What do you need me for?" Tristan asked, heading back into the main workroom. He threw himself on a low couch, one arm and leg slung over the back as he considered Reece.

"Just like that?"

"I'll do anything for Sierra. You need me, just say so."

Hands in his pockets, Reece rocked back on his heels and considered how much to share. He didn't want to spill Sierra's secrets, but he could use an expert eye.

"I need you to look over the shots. Give me your opinion. Any clues. Any insights that will help me nail the bastard who's doing this."

He didn't mention Sierra's uncle. No point leaving a witness in case he had to go kill the old guy. But if the finger pointed toward Sierra's past, and he figured it had a fifty-fifty chance of heading that way, Reece was going to be hunting down that son of a bitch. He couldn't do anything to change her past, and as much as he hated it, he understood her reasoning that he leave it alone. But if Donovan was behind this, that made it the present. And if that was the case, all bets were off.

Tristan swung his feet to the floor, and in one smooth move, slid to his feet and held out his hand.

"You got the pictures on you?"

"At my office." Reece waited for the protest or conditions.

But none came. The photographer picked up the phone, punched in a number and waited. "I have to cancel today's shoot. Reschedule." He paused, then, "I don't care. Get someone else to take it, then. I'll let you know when I'll be back."

He tossed the phone to the desk and faced Reece.

"Let's rock."

SIERRA WAS STILL seething the next day. But she wasn't letting it slow her down. No way, baby. She strode through the refurbished Victorian mansion, her Ferragamo slingbacks snapping sassily on the parquet floor. She'd be damned if she'd allow Reece's stubborn melodrama to affect her ability to do her job.

With that in mind, she made her way through the waitstaff, the decorators and the orchestra checking in. Her stress mounted with each encounter. The tea party for Family was in an hour and she hadn't been able to check off one damned thing on her list. Not unusual, given the scope and size of this two-hundred-guest event. But the stress she was having was out of her norm. Usually Sierra took it all in stride, passed out encouragement and pepped everyone up as she double-checked and organized the last-minute details. Today she was too overwhelmed to do more than sigh and shrug.

Today was the final event for Family. She and Belle had done it. Despite the enormity of the client's demands and the stressful stalker drama, they'd reached the end of their first integrated corporate launch. And it had been a huge success.

Which meant she'd be able to cut Belle a huge check for her portion of the company. To revisit the lawyers and draw up full partnership papers. She'd finally be on equal footing. She wished she felt an ounce of the excitement she'd always imagined over that scenario. But she was numb.

Sierra checked with the electricians wiring for the slide-show, then headed for the main event space to see if the florists had delivered and set up the arrangements.

The ballroom was done. Round, linen-covered tables were scattered around the room with their lush floral bouquets. Each was set for the Queen's tea, with bone china and silver tiered trays. Right now, the tiers were filled with flowers, but if the caterer got her act together, they'd be swapped for canapés and savories when the event started. On one wall was a widescreen monitor, on the other a small podium with a ten-foot blowup of the debut magazine cover.

Thank God, Sierra sighed. Something she could check off as complete.

"You don't have to do it all yourself," Belle said softly behind her.

Sierra started and her pen ripped through the checklist. She gave Belle a grimace and shrugged. "I'm just doing my job. Nothing's coming together yet, though. There's so much riding on this last event. Our future is teetering here, and we don't even have the appetizers ready."

"It'll be fine," Belle assured her.

"My job is to make sure it is, to handle all these details," Sierra shot back, flipping the pages on her clipboard, trying to focus.

"Hey," Belle said quietly.

Glancing over at her partner, Sierra saw the concern and love in Belle's gaze. Instantly, her own eyes filled with tears and her lower lip trembled so hard she couldn't get words past it.

"Oh, shit," she breathed, trying to hold the breakdown at bay.

"Sweetie?"

"No," Sierra said, holding up a hand to stop Belle from touching her. No hugs. No sympathy. She couldn't handle it. "I'll be okay."

Her heart ached at the look on Belle's face. She could see the worry clearly. And underneath was fear. Fear caused by the stalker, fear for Sierra's safety. Fear Belle had been keeping to herself so she wouldn't add to Sierra's stress.

"Is there anything I can do?" Belle murmured, her foot tapping nervously. Sierra knew it was all Belle could do to keep from pacing the floor.

Why was she making her friend pay for past ugliness that she wasn't even a part of? Belle had never let her down. Never screwed her over or hurt her. And how did Sierra repay that? With mistrust?

How unfair was that? How wrong? Was Reece right? Had burying her head in the sand, hiding from her past, been a part of these nightmares?

And why was she hiding from Belle? Sure, it'd made sense to keep her ugly home life a secret in boarding school. But ten years later? Belle was her best friend. She trusted her. And maybe it was time to prove that.

Sierra took a deep breath again, pressing her hand to her stomach to calm the churning. "Can we talk later?" she asked. "After the gig? I need to share with you. Just…share something."

"Are you okay?" A million questions swirled in Belle's eyes. Sierra could almost hear her mind working.

"I'll be fine," was all Sierra said. Now that she'd decided to open up, she could wait. An intense pressure against the back of her neck that she hadn't even realized was there suddenly eased. She could breathe now.

"Sure," Belle agreed slowly. Her green eyes, so reflective of her every thought, glistened in concern and love. "Whatever you need. We'll do a pitcher or three of margaritas and talk."

The catering staff started making their rounds and the band entered, setting up behind the podium. The head caterer headed their way with her usual pre-event taste test of the dessert.

Chocolate, she claimed, made any occasion smoother. Sierra was slowly regaining her taste for the treat.

Toby came in, camera bags and tripod over his shoulder. He explained that Tristan was tied up and would be a little late, but that he'd get the shots set. Since the photographer's actual contract with Family was over and this was just for Tristan's portfolio, Sierra didn't object.

Belle took a deep breath, pasted on her Kewpie-doll smile and pointed to the garden doors where the first stage of the party would take place. "Well, this is our last gig for these people. Let's knock their shoes off."

Three hours later, Sierra was pretty sure they'd done just that. After a meet and greet in the garden, the Family entourage, sponsors and guests had moved into the ballroom for high tea. The orchestra played softly, a calm backdrop to the genteel setting. The guests had taken the theme to heart, the men in suits and the women in flowing dresses and floppy hats.

Toby moved among the guests, silently shooting pictures. Sierra wondered briefly how he could see through the curtain of flat-ironed hair hanging over his eyes.

"Kitchen's under control," she murmured to Belle as she joined her partner in the doorway to watch the crowd take their seats and fill their plates with scones.

"Corinne is due to speak in five minutes," Belle murmured back as she glanced at her own clipboard. "We ran a sound check just before they came in to tea, so it's all covered."

Sierra signaled the pianist, letting her know they needed to segue from background music to Family's theme song. That would let Corinne know to start making her way to the podium. The slideshow was currently playing on the opposite wall.

One speech, the chocolate course and a little more socializing, and they were done.

Sierra grinned at Belle. Against the odds, they'd rocked this.

She'd never admit it, but the idea of working for such an archconservative group had worried her. Throw in pervy stalkers and the miserable joys of a failed love affair and it had been one hell of a challenge.

But they'd done it.

Belle gasped. Sierra shot her a look. Her friend was pure white, her eyes horrified.

Her shock was echoed by the rest of the room. Trying to see the cause, Sierra stared over the sea of big floaty hats and chiffon. The screen against the far wall caught her eye.

The slideshow had stopped. Before, it had flashed colorful ads for the magazine and TV spots, interspersed with promotional shots and candids of the Family team.

Now the wall was covered by a full color shot of Sierra, naked in bed with Corinne and six burly guys in chains and black leather.

Her head spun. Her stomach threatened to revolt. She tried to catch her breath. Slowly, every eye in the room turned from the horror on the screen. Searching, seeking, then landing on her.

Sierra wished she were a fainting kind of gal. The idea of passing out and hitting her head on some sharp object, maybe sustaining a nasty concussion, held a great appeal right that moment.

But she couldn't even faint. Instead she stood there, her vintage Ferragamo slingbacks glued to the marble floor. She couldn't move, couldn't breathe. All she could do was stare at the ugliness splashed in its computer-enhanced wonder on the opposite wall and watch her world fall apart. Someone—Belle, she figured—grabbed her arm and pulled her out of the room.

Sierra stumbled along, unable to stop looking over her shoulder at the picture.

"Get that off the screen," Belle hissed to somebody. "I don't care how. Cut the power to the whole damned building if you have to."

"Oh, God," she breathed. "He did it. He did it."

She couldn't think straight. Everyone was staring. Judging. Believing her to be the ugly slut on the screen. Believing the worst. Judging her.

Even here, hidden in the little anteroom that the servers used for linens, she could feel the stares. Could still see the image of her face on somebody else's naked body.

"I've got to get out of here," she said. Frantically looking for an escape, she forced herself to keep breathing. But the walls were closing in and she had to go. Now.

"Sierra, you can't. You can't drive right now. Just wait a second, I'll figure it out."

"No," she said, her voice rising. "I need to go. I really do. Now. I'm sorry."

So sorry.

"Hey, I'll take her."

Sierra raised devastated eyes to Toby. She felt Belle's arm curve protectively around her back, but knew it wasn't enough. She had to get out of here.

"That's okay," Belle started to say. "I've called Mitch, he'll be here in a few minutes…"

"I don't want to wait a few minutes," Sierra murmured. Her hands shook, nausea curdling her stomach. "I want to—need to—go now."

Without another word, she patted Belle's hand and stepped away before her friend could hug her. No. She didn't want to be touched, to be comforted. She felt dirty. Filthy. She had to get out of here and a few minutes were too long to wait.

"C'mon, Toby," she said. "I need a ride home."

"YOU'RE SURE he's here?" Reece asked as he climbed the steps to the mansion. He was genuinely grateful to have Tristan at his side. The guy, he'd discovered, had one hell of an eye and a quick mind.

"He said he'd cover the event himself," Tristan said, his tone low and angry. Oddly enough, his fury helped blunt Reece's own. Almost as if the other man would lose it big-time if Reece showed even a hint of the rage pounding through him.

"Don't let your suspicions get the best of you," Reece cautioned as they reached the doors. He laid a hand on Tristan's shoulder, stopping the other man. Meeting the emotion churning in the guy's eyes, he shook his head. "Seriously. We don't know that he's guilty."

"*I* know." The photographer tried to shake him off, but Reece didn't let go.

"I realize you're pissed. I understand you think there is enough evidence here to point the finger. But you need to listen. We can't go in there and get ugly. For one thing, if it is him, Sierra could be in danger. For another, whether it is or not, if we screw up her event she'll kick both our asses."

Tristan's lips twitched, some of the hard edge leaving his eyes. "You know her pretty well."

Reece grimaced. A lot of good that knowledge had done him, considering how badly he'd screwed up. He couldn't focus on that right now, though. All he could do was his damnedest to handle this case, then fix things.

"Maybe," he acknowledged. "At least I know her enough to realize we have to keep our cool."

He waited for the photographer to nod his agreement before letting him go. Then Reece led the way through the antique glass doors with Tristan by his side.

As they headed down the hall in the direction of the noise, he imagined the look on Sierra's face when he walked in. Nothing like giving her visual proof that he'd listened to her to smooth the waters. At least, he hoped so. And maybe he was counting on the fact that it was a public venue and a client event to keep her from instantly kicking him out, too.

Solving the case would just be the icing on the cake.

They reached the ballroom and all thought of icing, cake and even winning flew from his mind. Chaos reigned.

Heart racing, Reece scanned the room. Where the hell was Sierra? He couldn't see a damned thing through all the gaudy hats and waving arms.

Just as he was about to shove his way through the crowd, his cell phone rang. Lightning fast, he grabbed it and answered, not even bothering to check the caller ID.

"Carter."

"We've got a problem." It was Paul, the security guy he'd left in charge.

"No shit. I'm here. Where are you?"

Before he'd finished asking, he saw the burly bald man at the far end of the hall, standing guard in a doorway. Reece didn't waste any more words, pushing his way through the crowd. Tristan, he knew, was right on his heels.

He crossed through the cacophony of raised, angry voices. Paul tried to hand him a digital card but Reece waved him off.

"What the hell happened?" he asked, focusing on the only person in the room he recognized, Belle.

"The pervert struck again," she spat ferociously. Reece watched a couple of the guys who'd been arguing with her back off at her obvious anger. "The sicko got a hold of our slideshow. In the middle of the presentation, another one of his doctored photos froze on the screen. Perfect timing to do exactly what he'd promised. Ruin the event and our reputation."

"How?"

She shoved her hands through her already disheveled curls before throwing them in the air. "I don't know. You screened the shots before we arrived. Your security guy was here all along. I have no idea how someone got that disgusting thing past us, but they did."

"Where's Sierra?" he asked, looking around. God, she must be devastated. He needed to get to her. To hold her and make sure she was okay.

"She froze. Oh, God, Reece, she was so horrified. So hurt." Tears streamed down Belle's cheeks. Unable to stop himself, Reece pulled her into his arms.

"It's okay," he murmured against her hair. Seeing his cousin run through the door, he sighed and happily handed her over to her man. "I'll take care of her. Just let me know where she is."

Belle looked up from Mitch's shoulder and sniffed. "Like I said, she freaked. She had to get out of here. She was already upset, then, I don't know, something sent her over the top. She just said she had to get out. I didn't try to stop her."

"She went home? She was that upset and you let her drive? What the hell were you thinking? Why didn't you go with her?" Anger made Reece's words harsher than he'd intended. He ignored the sharp look Mitch shot him and focused on Belle's frown.

"I think she was going home," she said with a grimace. "She's okay, though. I wouldn't have let her leave on her own."

Relief poured through Reece and he unfisted his hands. He glanced around, realizing she'd had no choice. He recognized the ashen-faced old lady as the top-dog client, and the grim-faced guys around her were probably legal. Belle had obviously stuck around to deal with the drama.

And good friend that she was, she'd saved Sierra the stress by sending her away. He squeezed her arm in gratitude.

"Who's she with?" he asked, glancing over Tristan's shoulder at the incriminating evidence the photographer had pulled up on the mini-viewing screen of his digital camera.

Spying the old lady sporting a conical leather bra, Reece grimaced and realized why she looked so freaked. Not only had her event been ruined, she'd been a part of the floor show.

"Toby took her," Belle said, her words partly muffled against Mitch's chest. "He hurried her out right after the picture flashed and got stuck on the screen. Thankfully before the full uproar hit."

Reece didn't hear anything past the first sentence. Despite his caution to Tristan about unfounded accusations, his gut knew the photographer's assistant was the stalker.

Turning on his booted heel, he yelled to Tristan to explain and sprinted out of the room.

Scared like he'd never been in all the years spent risking his life, Reece ran as fast as he could. He hoped like hell the idiot played true to form. Possibilities flashed through his mind like a horror movie. Reece forced himself to shove aside his terror for Sierra and focused on the only thing he could.

Saving the woman he loved.

Training and brains. They were the only weapons he had with him.

13

"WHY ARE WE here?" Sierra asked as Toby pulled up to the studio. Irritation fought with anger when she realized she wasn't home.

She'd barely paid attention to the drive, climbing in his ancient Honda and closing her eyes to try and block out the horrible images. Only by focusing all her energy on deep belly breaths had she managed to keep from puking over the dingy gray interior of her chariot.

"Tristan texted me," Toby said, turning off the ignition and giving her a quick look through the curtain of hair covering half his face. "He's got a problem. You don't mind if we run in, do you? It shouldn't take more than a few minutes, but I don't want to leave you alone out here."

Sierra shook herself as if she were coming out of a bad dream. All she wanted to do was go home, climb into bed and pull the covers over her head. She knew that whining she had plenty of problems of her own was immature, but dammit, she didn't feel like helping anyone right now, not even Tristan. She just wanted to be alone, to hide and lick her wounds.

But Toby was already unlocking the door to the dark studio. With a reluctant sigh, she followed him, noting he locked the doors behind them. "Afraid those rabid women in big hats are going to hunt me down with teaspoons?" she joked unenthusiastically.

Toby snorted, but shook his head. "Nah. Tristan gets pissy when I don't lock the doors after hours."

Sierra smirked tiredly at the idea of the mellow photographer being termed pissy.

"What's Tristan's problem?" she asked, needing to focus on something other than the humiliation of that photo. Every time she blinked, she saw her altered self on display for more than two hundred people. "Some hot model cornered him and demanded his virtue but he didn't have any left to give her?"

She winced at the lousy joke. She needed to stop. That hadn't even been worthy of the pity laugh Toby offered.

"Actually, he's in jail," Toby said as they reached the end of the long hallway and entered the huge, cavernous office. As usual, it reflected a balance between Tristan's lack of organization and Toby's refusal to allow a mess.

It wasn't until Sierra dropped to the settee that Toby's words sank in.

"What?" she yelped. What was going on today? Were the planets aligned upside down or something? "What the hell was Tristan arrested for?"

Toby leaned back against the desk with a scowl. He stared at his sneaker-clad feet for a second, then met her gaze. Sierra caught her breath at the look in his eyes. A twisted, angry sort of pleasure. She frowned. Something wasn't right.

"Because of you, actually," he said slowly. "Your boyfriend was here the other day. He poked around, asked a bunch of questions."

Sierra growled low in her throat. Unable to relax, she stood. She wanted nothing more than to kick off her shoes and pace. She didn't know why, but she couldn't.

Nerves. Her nerves were shot after all the crap of the day. It had to be that.

Sierra tried to believe her own bullshit, but she knew

nerves didn't explain the little hairs prickling on the back of her neck.

"Look, let's go to the cops," she said. Even more than she'd wanted out of the mansion, she wanted out of this room. It had to be the proximity to photographs or something. After all, she'd spent hours here in the past and never felt this creeped out. "I know it's not Tristan. I'll talk to them. I'll explain. Post bail. Something. We need to get him out of there."

Something like a sneer flashed over Toby's face, but it was gone too fast for Sierra to figure out.

"You're sure it's not him?" he asked quietly.

"Of course I am. Anyone who knows him knows his aversion to technology. The guy only got a cell phone last year and that's because you nagged him crazy over it. He's not the stalker."

Toby was silent.

"This isn't the first time someone's messed with my pictures, played this game," she admitted desperately. "It's been going on for a couple of months now. The cops know about it. They have the pictures. We have to go talk to them."

"I don't think that's going to help Tristan," Toby mused morosely. He shifted, just a little. Now he stood between her and the phone. Unintentionally, she was sure. But she felt weird. Vulnerable. She wished like crazy she hadn't left her purse and cell phone back at the mansion.

"Look, even if the cops don't realize Tristan's a technophobe, we can take his portfolio in. That'll help," she insisted.

"Half his shots are nudes," Toby pointed out. "If that picture of you is the kind of thing they're accusing him of, that's hardly going to help his case."

"But it will," Sierra contended. "As soon as they see the differences it'll be obvious."

Toby frowned. "How?"

"I don't know," she admitted, feeling frustrated.

Even nerves couldn't keep her still any longer, and she began to pace. Her shoes made it impossible to go as fast as she needed, but at least she was moving and could think again.

"Look," Toby pointed out, "whoever did this is clever. Really smart. I mean, you had security there at the tea and they got around it. They doctored the photo card, they got both you and that old lady into that shot and made it look totally real. Right down to the expressions on your faces."

Sierra winced, waving her hand to try and fend off the image of her and the geriatric kinkfest. God, it was like someone accusing her of sleeping her way to her jobs.

Then Reece had Tristan arrested. Sierra kicked at a bolt of fabric, fury filling her as she realized that he had yet again totally ignored her.

She paused and forced herself to ask the question that had nagged at the back of her mind for the last day.

Why? He had to have a reason. She pressed her fingers to the throbbing behind her eyes, as if relieving the pressure would lessen her confusion.

She'd wanted to blame him. To use his relentless pursuit of the truth as an excuse to hide from the facts. She'd been terrified to consider that someone close to her—someone in this new, carefully insulated life she'd created for herself—could be behind the ugliness.

Reece had told her she had to quit hiding her head in the sand and deal with reality. And she would. Just as soon as she figured out what it was.

Pacing, she tried to concentrate on what she knew.

Fact. Reece wasn't the kind of guy to make sloppy accusations. So if he'd told the cops that Tristan was behind the stalking, there was some concrete reason for it.

Another fact. Whoever it was had an axe to grind with her,

with Family or with both. As much as she'd believed—wanted to believe—it was her uncle, there was nothing for him to gain in this. But Tristan? She didn't know why he'd been in jail, but she knew he couldn't be behind all this. And if he was, why had Toby brought her here instead of to the police station?

"You gotta admit, that picture wasn't bad." Toby's claim pulled her out of her reverie. Sierra shot him a questioning look. "I mean, it was nasty, yeah. But the composition, the contrasts, they were solid."

"Actually no. The pictures—all of them, including today's— are really crappy." Sierra frowned absently as she paced. "The lighting, the angles. Totally amateur. If you'd asked me yesterday, I'd have sworn Tristan couldn't take pictures that bad if he tried."

Toby made a sound, but she didn't stop. Her brain was trying to grab something. It was right there on the edge of her awareness and she didn't want to lose it.

"An amateur," she repeated to herself as she worked her way around the perimeter of the room. "Little or no photographic abilities. Fair computer skills."

Which was why it could be Peter. But the shots, the angles— they'd be hard for him to get. She mentally flipped through the recent photos. The ones that had scared her so much because they were of her living her life. From the one of her being eaten by an eight-foot bronze vagina to the one of her driving on the freeway, they'd all had something in common.

"Side angles—poorly framed shots," she muttered. Why was that nagging at her? "Where have I seen that mistake before?"

"What are you talking about?" Toby snapped. Sierra's gaze flew to the younger man. No longer lounging, he stood in the middle of the room with his hands fisted on his hips. Anger and something more subtle, more threatening, etched lines in his face. He shoved his hair out of his eyes to glare at her.

Her pace slowed, then stopped. She felt like she was tiptoeing through a lightning storm, but didn't know why. She wasn't sure what or where the strike was coming from, but knew she needed to be careful.

"I'm talking about the stalker pictures," she said carefully.

"You didn't learn anything, did you?" He glared, his hate-filled eyes sending pure loathing her way. His hair, usually so flat and smooth, now stood every which way.

For the first time, she saw both his eyes at once. His angular bangs always made her think that he was trying to look around a corner.

Side angles.

"Oh my God," she breathed. "It's you?"

He snorted. "Took you long enough."

"Why?" Confusion, fury, terror. They all tangled together in her guts, tying her in knots. She couldn't move. Couldn't even pace. She felt frozen and helpless.

She wondered if this was how Alice had felt when she'd tripped through the looking glass—dazed, confused and totally out of her element.

"I don't understand—" She stopped talking at the depth of anger in his eyes. Deep breath. She took a step back toward the door. He scowled. Sierra froze.

"I didn't learn," she agreed, falling into the passive role she'd learned so well as a teenager. "Maybe you can help me figure it out?"

"And you think you're so smart. So much better than everyone else."

She really needed to work on her image issues. Her aunt thought her the greatest slut of the Western world and now this from Toby? At least nobody was clueing in to her real issues. Except for Reece.

Reece.

As if the sanity plug had been pulled, Toby went off.

"I hate bitches who think they know everything," he ranted. "You. My mother. Dumb chicks at clubs. Stupid models. All so damned superior. All sluts. All superior know-it-all sluts who can't appreciate true talent and individuality."

He was sputtering now, his words hard to follow. He started punctuating his rant by throwing things off the desk, tossing office supplies and books against the walls.

"Nobody appreciates. Nobody gets real creativity. All your stupid excuses are just fear. Inferiority. You're all scared." Sierra backed up another step, unable to deny that he was, indeed, scaring the hell out of her. "Tristan listens to all these dumb bitches instead of me. I'm the one here taking care of him. I'm the one who sees his potential. I'm the only one who understands him. But you, you corner him into crappy contracts and he does it out of friendship. He listens to you when he should listen to me."

Sierra stood across from a crazy kid, his eyes wild and little bits of spittle flying from his mouth as he raged and paced. She was scared to death. This guy had terrorized her. He had deliberately set out to make her life a living hell. To scare her and manipulate her and ruin her business.

If his pictures were anything to go by, he was a pervert with a yen for violence. If his rantings were anything to go by, he was in love with Tristan and thought she stood in his way.

But a little bit of the horror that had dogged her for the last few months melted away.

Maybe she was as stupid as Toby thought.

Maybe just knowing who was behind the threats lifted the veil of terror. No more was there a shadowy boogeyman haunting her. It was a punk kid with a weird attention-getting scheme.

Maybe it was simple relief that her past was no longer her

present. That she didn't have to live in fear that the horrible accusations and ugliness she'd left behind would come back and
ruin what she'd created.

Or maybe, just maybe it was because she had complete faith
that Reece would be here anytime to end this joke of a drama.

She knew he'd figure it out. He'd refused to give up the case.
Firing him would only spur him on to prove her wrong, to
confirm his skill at his job.

She'd told him to drop it and he'd had Tristan arrested.

But he wouldn't stop there. He'd interview him. He'd ask
questions. He'd push and prod and probe and be a general pain
in the ass. Then he'd insist on coming here.

She wouldn't—couldn't—run away. She had to stand her
ground. All she had to do was keep Toby distracted until Reece
arrived. She watched him pace, manically punching furniture
and swearing as he went. Okay, so maybe she wasn't as
unafraid as she'd like. But as long as she told herself otherwise,
she could keep the panic at bay. Panic was a bigger threat to
her right now than the lunatic frothing at the mouth across from
her. She had to remember that.

"Why?" she asked again, hoping a little focus would calm
him down. "I don't get it. What's with the crappy pictures? The
stalker bit? The threats?"

His pale face flushed an ugly, mottled magenta. "I'm sick
and tired of you dissing my talent. Of not showing me the
proper respect."

Sierra gave a baffled laugh. "Respect? You're kidding, right?
I mean, you edited my head on backward in the first few
pictures. This was all some kind of joke, right?"

"Joke? The joke is that you waste Tristan on all these big
fancy-paying jobs. If you'd have given me a chance instead of
blowing me off, I could have taken over those stupid shoots,
left Tristan to follow his art. I could take the run-of-the-mill

pictures, digitize them, bring this studio out of the dark ages and into the techno age. But you've ruined it all for us."

"But…" Sierra shook her head in confusion. "Ignoring the fact that Tristan is a complete hetero, he's totally focused on his own vision of his business. I didn't twist his arm to work with me. He wanted to. Besides, he's a total technophobe. He's a photographic purist. If he had his way, he'd still use a darkroom."

"He's an artist," Toby repeated. Sierra wasn't sure what was freaking her out more—seeing both Toby's eyes at the same time, or witnessing the demented fury shining in them. "As soon as he's free from your stupid contract, your demands on his time, he'll be able to see and appreciate what I can offer him. He'll be able to see the digital benefits."

Sierra stared. He was kidding, right? She wished she could laugh. She wanted this to be a joke. Shock was fading like a misty fog in the sunshine. But without shock, fear was creeping in to take its place.

"It's all your fault," Toby said as he stomped from one desk to the other, pausing to kick a chair aside. Sierra jumped as the wheeled seat flew across the room. To hell with standing her ground. Heart pounding, she took one tiny step closer to the door. Toby glared. She froze, not breathing again until he resumed his frantic march across the room.

Her stomach knotted so tight she could barely breathe. Her chances of escaping unscathed were starting to look slim to none.

"Let me get this straight," she said slowly, unable to stop herself. "You have spent the last couple months terrorizing me. Following me around with a camera, spending hours doctoring perverted pictures, sending me threats. And all because…what again? Because I hired Tristan?"

Toby sneered. "You sound just like my mother. Trying to make it like I'm unreasonable or stupid."

She knew very little about Toby's personal life, but wasn't his mom dead? Her stomach churned, and black spots danced in front of her eyes. He wasn't a Norman Bates, was he? Then she remembered she'd met his mom at Tristan's funky *Twelfth Night* costume party last year. Not dead, she remembered. Just hypercritical and extremely controlling of her very embarrassed son.

No wonder he was such a mess.

"Don't you realize they'll figure out it wasn't Tristan eventually?" she said faintly.

Spittle gathered at the corner of Toby's mouth as if he were a mad dog. "Tristan? Give me a break. I don't give a damn if they think it's him or not."

Sierra frowned.

"Didn't you say he'd been arrested? Don't you realize that as soon as they realize it's not him, they'll look elsewhere? Or that when I get out of here, I'll tell someone the truth?"

His grin was pure evil. Ugly, mean and terrifying. Sierra's hands started shaking. Her knees turned to jelly.

"Oh my God. You're planning to...what? Kill me?" Well, shit. Sierra knew the fear was there. It was a living thing, surrounding her, seeping into her skin. But for one brief second, all she felt was anger. She wasn't going to let some obnoxious kid take her life away from her. She had things to do. Reece in particular.

"Overreact much?" Toby sneered. He was good at that. She shoved her hands into her pockets to keep herself from reaching out to smack the obnoxious look off his face.

Her hand brushed something cool and hard. Shock and hope jarred her already stretched-out nerves as her fingers closed around her cell phone.

"If you're not going to hurt me, what are you planning to do?" she asked, trying to keep the anxious hopefulness out of her voice. She had her phone. She could reach Belle. The cops. Someone. Even as she thought that, she knew the only person she wanted—needed—was Reece.

All she had to do was let him know where she was. He'd take care of the rest.

"I'm planning to do exactly what I've planned all along," Toby told her as he moved through the room like a frenzied thief who couldn't find anything to steal. He tossed things off chairs, over-turned pillows and opened drawers, searching for something.

"I'm going to blackmail you," he said slowly, his frown telling her he was frustrated at not finding whatever it was he was looking for.

"Blackmail me?" What? How? Sierra made a show of shifting from foot to foot as if her heels hurt her, using the movement to inch a little closer to the door. "With what?"

She considered running. Maybe if she kicked off her heels she'd have a chance? A brief mournful sigh over the possible loss of a killer pair of Ferragamos. It wasn't worry over the sling-backs that stopped her, though. It was the fact that if she took off, he'd catch her. Almost guaranteed. And then she'd tip her hand.

Sierra swallowed hard. Did it matter if she tipped it? Trying to decide, she edged a little closer to the door.

"I blew your deal with that uptight, holier-than-thou company," Toby pointed out, the triumph in his voice like a little bully announcing that he'd just smashed someone's toy. "I have the pictures all ready, everything set to send out to your entire client list."

Sierra froze. "What?"

"Yep. I figured I'd send you copies along with a demand for ten grand. I've already proved what I can do with my editing program. I planned to send the pictures to a select number of clients, the *L.A. Times* and then hit the paparazzi."

Sierra wanted to tell him what a stupid plan it was. To point out that she'd never cave to some pitiful blackmail scheme he'd dreamed up over his Fruity Pebbles.

Except she couldn't.

Because he was right. He'd put her on edge enough over the pictures that she'd have no problem throwing something his way to make them stop. Hell, she'd spent the last ten years doing it with her family and all she had at stake there was having to deal with their rotten selves in her life again. Toby had a much stronger hand.

Especially after that picture today. She remembered the image of Corinne in black leather, the setup making it look as if she and Sierra were kinky lovers. Yeah, he'd already cost her one client, damaged her reputation and, if Corinne followed through with the threats she'd been sputtering when Sierra left, embroiled Eventfully Yours in an ugly lawsuit.

Seeming to read her thoughts, Toby grinned. It was that boyish, kid-next-door smile that made it all so surreal. "Gotcha."

That smile, that little-boy look. Now she remembered. "I know you," she murmured. "You were…"

"Yep. My momma worked for your uncle. I used to play in the kitchen when she couldn't get a babysitter."

"Did he put you up to this?"

Toby laughed, a bitter sound. "Hardly. He didn't see me any more than you did. But I listened to him, whenever he'd come to our house at night and bring my mom presents. He'd say they were from you. I didn't get it until a few years ago. Then when I realized how you were ruining my future with Tristan, I figured I'd take a page out of good ole Uncle Peter's book."

He knew her secrets. Knew her uncle had hit her up for money. Did he know she'd been charged with assault? Had he listened to her uncle's rants about what a slut she was? Was that why he'd picked sexual pictures to ruin her? Her biggest fears were now right here in her face. But this time she couldn't run from them. Couldn't hide. Instead, Sierra faked a casual shrug. "It didn't work, though."

"That's okay. There's always plan B."

She grimaced. That didn't sound very promising. At least, not for her. She glanced at the door, trying to gauge distance. Toby rolled his eyes and gave her a "Yeah, right" look, then grabbed her arm and pushed her to the opposite side of the room.

"I'm faster than you are, and if you try to run I'll hurt you. Just sit down and shut up. If you move, I'll hear you."

He waited until she'd lowered herself to the couch, then, his eyes still glued on her, he backed toward the storage room. Still facing her, he shoved the curtain aside and glanced over his shoulder.

"Don't move," he cautioned again. Then he turned and quickly dove behind the curtain. His feet, clad in beat-up basketball shoes, never moved more than a few inches from the opening. There was no way she'd escape before he heard her.

One eye glued to the movement behind the curtain, she slid her hand into the pocket of her jacket and pulled out her cell phone. Cursing silently at her slow texting speed, she sent Reece what she hoped was an SOS.

Trapped @ studio. Help.

Toby pushed his way back through the curtain, incongruously holding yards of filmy blue fabric. With fear slamming her heart against her rib cage, Sierra dropped the phone into her pocket and folded her fingers in front of her. And hoped like hell that pressing the little button on the side had silenced both her ringtone and her texting volume.

Reece had to get the message. She just hoped he was somewhere in town and that she hadn't sent him off on a wild-goose chase after her uncle.

God, why hadn't she listened to him? Why hadn't she allowed for the possibility that she could be wrong? Or at least been open to Reece's point of view? Nope, she'd had to be right. Had to fire him in all her self-justified, righteous indignation. She'd acted just as immaturely as the spoiled man-boy in front of her, currently creating a rope out of a length of twisted fabric.

"Move," Toby ordered, pointing to the chair he'd kicked across the room, then wrapped in fabric. If she sat, she'd be mummified. No thank you.

"I don't think so," she told him, standing up but stepping away from the chair in question. "I'd have to be as stupid as you claim to let you tie me up."

He heaved a put-upon sigh that clearly said she was the biggest pain in the ass he could imagine. It would do her aunt proud. Then he pulled out a knife. Sierra's blood stopped. She fixated on the glinting silver metal, remembering how a matching knife had skewered her front door.

"Look, I'm probably not going to hurt you." He grinned at her incredulous look and shrugged. "You do what I say, you'll be okay. You ruined my blackmail plan so I need to get the money somewhere. Your bank account will work fine. I'll transfer it here on the computer, then leave. You'll be found. Eventually."

He made it sound so reasonable, Sierra almost stepped forward. She'd spent years doing just what her uncle said. Letting herself be tied up, trapped. Held prisoner by someone else's ugly agenda.

Fury, this time at herself, flamed inside her gut. It burned away a layer of the fear, giving her a crystal clear picture of just what a total wienie she'd be if she gave in. She'd be exactly what her aunt and uncle, exactly what Toby, claimed. Stupid and pitiful. A victim.

"No."

It was hard to tell who was more shocked by her refusal. Her or Toby.

"I'm going to ruin your ass," he promised, waving the knife. His words were menacing, but his eyes puzzled. Guarded. And the most dangerous she'd seen since he'd shoved the hair off his face. "If you don't sit down right now, I'm going to hurt you. Then I'll not only take the money, I'll send these pictures and ruin your reputation. Destroy your business. Make your life a living hell."

He was promising everything her relatives had and more. And his ability to pull it off was even greater. His threat was real and solid, where theirs was nebulous and weak. And she'd always given in to them.

But she was through being bullied. Sierra crossed her arms over her chest, her fingers quivering against her biceps as she shook her head.

"No," she repeated. It didn't matter if her voice trembled. That didn't lessen her determination one iota. "You're not getting a single penny from me. If you want to send out those pictures, you go ahead. I'll deny they're real. I won't let you bully me or push me around."

"You don't get a choice."

"The hell I don't."

Apparently tired of waiting for her to obey, he leaped forward and grabbed her arm. She kicked him as hard as she could with the wicked point of her shoe. He grunted, bending double in pain, but his grip on her wrist didn't lessen.

Using her best defense, she brought her knee up hard and sharp. The knife hit the floor with a clatter. Toby twisted, yelping in fury. Releasing her arm, he swung his fist and sent her flying backward.

Her face on fire, Sierra stumbled, falling into the chair. Before she could blink the pain from her eyes or wipe the blood from her lip, he jumped on her with a growl of rage. Then, seeing the blood on her chin, he shook his head like a wet dog. Hissing through his teeth, he looped a length of tulle around her throat, then shoved her into the chair.

Tears burned her eyes, but Sierra refused to let them fall. Dammit, this standing-her-ground shit sucked. Her cowboy had better hurry up before she seriously regretted trying to be brave.

"There," Toby growled as he finished knotting the fabric at her ankles. "Now you'll pay."

14

"TOBY," she pleaded through a swollen bottom lip as he looped a soft pink feather boa around her wrists to hold them behind her back. He wouldn't look at her. Apparently the blood had freaked him out a little, because while he was careful to tie her securely, he seemed to be making sure he didn't cause her further injury. He'd also kicked the knife across the room, where it sat in ugly warning under his desk.

"You can't do this," she appealed. "You won't get away with it. Seriously, after you take my money, what are you going to do? Run away? Someone will find you eventually."

"Nobody's going to find me," he insisted as he came around to face her, his eyes getting that wild look again. Sierra gulped. "I've got it planned. My plan's worked perfectly so far, and the rest of it will, too."

"Did you plan to haul me here and tie me up with feathers?" she asked.

He glared. "No. Your boyfriend shouldn't have arrested Tristan. I can't let him take the fall for me, so I grabbed you so they'll know he's not guilty. Your asshole boyfriend made me mad, ruined my plans. All I needed were six more days, maybe four, and I'd have had everything ready. Damned assholes ruined it all."

Muttering threats and complaints, he turned away and flipped on the computer.

Despite the pain, she clenched her jaw against frustrated sobs. Why hadn't Reece listened to her? Maybe if she'd given him all the information early on, instead of hiding her dirty little secret away in shame, he could have solved this, could have saved her.

"Reece won't let you get away with this," she murmured.

Toby gave a dismissive shrug. "The cowboy's an idiot. He's just after getting into your pants. He won't be able to stop me."

"He'll not only stop you, I'll bet he's going to kick your ass when he does," she threatened hollowly.

A shadow moved by the door. Sierra's heart sputtered. Her eyes rounded. She almost cried out in relief.

"Actually, she'd win the bet."

Toby spun so fast the keyboard flew off the desk. Sierra just leaned back in the chair, closed her eyes in relief and let her fingers relax in the soft cloud of pink feathers.

Thank God.

REECE SHOVED his hands in his pockets and leaned one shoulder against the doorframe as he surveyed the scene in front of him. His stance was pure relaxation. His face was clear and slightly amused. His gut was churning with a combination of fear for Sierra and fury toward the asshole staring at him as if he'd sprouted horns under his hat.

"It's about time you got here," Sierra called from the fabric-bundled chair she was tied up in. He steeled himself, then let his gaze meet hers.

Violent rage bubbled inside him as he took in the blood on her chin, her swollen lip and the pain in her eyes. The creepy kid, smart enough to realize he was one step away from being beaten to a pulp, jumped behind Sierra to use her like a shield. He pulled her along, the chair's wheels scraping over the floor, until he reached the desk. Reece growled as the kid leaned over and grabbed a knife.

Reining in his emotions, Reece forced himself to ignore the knife and the kid. He looked into Sierra's eyes, trying to convey a sense of calm.

"Sorry it took so long," he told her quietly. "I had a few things to take care of."

"Like arresting the wrong person?" Toby taunted. "I can't believe you jumped the gun like that. I thought you were smarter."

Shocked, Reece raised a brow at Sierra. Her sigh and eye roll told him that yes, indeed, this kid was a complete idiot. Great. The only thing worse than dealing with a crazy criminal was a stupid one.

And this stupid one had a knife on Sierra. Reece calculated the distance, how fast he could grab the kid's neck. Too big a risk. He couldn't manhandle him. Yet. So he'd have to outsmart him.

"Nah, actually Tristan and I have been working together," he informed the kid. "He's talking to the cops now. Showing them all the evidence, making a statement." Reece paused for effect, then shot the twerp a vicious grin. "You know, making sure they have everything they need to arrest your sorry little ass."

It was a toss-up as to who looked more shocked—Toby or Sierra.

With a yelp of rage, the twerp shoved the knife beneath Sierra's chin, the sound of the fabric ripping beneath the blade almost overpowering Sierra's gasp. Reece forced himself not to jump forward. He needed to get the kid to let go of the knife.

Then he could beat the crap out of him.

"How dare you! You ruined it all. You turned Tristan against me. I hate you. Her. Everyone." Spinning around, he stabbed the knife into the desk. Then Toby started ranting. His words became disjointed as he kicked over the computer stand. Reece winced, knowing he needed the computer as evidence.

But that wasn't as important as saving Sierra. With the knife out of play for the moment and the kid focused on his meltdown, Reece focused on Sierra. He knew if he moved, the kid would notice. Would turn and have that knife back in his hand before she was safe. That meant it was all up to her. God, could she do it? Could she take the chance?

He knew she must have been devastated by her ruined event. Then to be hauled off here, terrorized and hurt. He was afraid of what he'd see in her eyes. Instead of terror or tears, he saw annoyance and relief in the blue depths. God, what a woman.

She winked and blew him a kiss. Then with a roll of her eyes, she inclined her head toward Toby and raised both brows as if to say, "Can you believe it?"

Reece tried to tell her with his eyes and subtle finger movements what he wanted her to do. He'd watch Toby while she inched her way toward him. The angle she was at meant she could only watch one of them, not both. She'd have to trust him completely. A scary thing since the lunatic was within inches of that knife, and had a pseudo leash around her neck. Could she?

Her acknowledgment was tiny, barely a flick of her lashes. He could see the fear in her eyes, but also the pure steel. It was obvious she wasn't about to let this kid win. Reece almost grinned, but Toby had stopped his desk-pounding tantrum and was now glaring directly at him. Luckily, he was also taking the bait. The fabric, yards long, was slack and loose in his fingers.

"You did this," the kid accused, his eyes wild. "All my work, all my planning, you ruined it."

Reece inclined his head, not looking at Sierra. Instead he kept his eyes locked on the kid. Kept his look taunting and confident. He wanted Toby's complete attention.

"I did," Reece lied. "I knew it was you all along. I just wanted to get enough evidence to hang you. To make sure you couldn't wiggle out of paying for what you've done."

Toby twisted, grabbed the monitor from the desk and heaved it across the room. It might have had a bigger impact if it had gone more than two feet.

But the move yanked Sierra's chair back a few inches. Reece jumped forward, but Toby's glare stopped him cold. He shifted his gaze, just a little, and saw that Sierra was okay. Better yet, she'd managed to free her hands. Wrists still tangled in pink feathers, she held the material away from her throat so it didn't choke her. She gave a quick little shake of her head to let him know that Toby hadn't hurt her.

"The cops have all the pictures. Tristan even backed up the programs and files off that computer this morning—took those in as evidence, too," Reece said, needing to egg the kid on a little more, keep his eyes on Reece instead of Sierra as she clawed free of the leash.

"You're lying. Tristan wouldn't turn on me. He wouldn't help you." Saliva dripped down his scrawny chin like foam, hate and triumph mingling in his eyes. Reece watched those eyes, seeing the decision there, the preparation. "You've blown it, cowboy. You and the slut will both pay for your lies. For ruining my plans."

"Oh, now that was your last mistake," Reece promised. "I don't take kindly to you calling Sierra names."

"What're you going to do about it?"

"Kick your ass, of course."

In a quick, cutting motion he slashed his hand to the side, indicating Sierra should move. She threw off the bindings in a blur. He heard the chair slide across the floor just as Toby launched himself across the room.

Reece caught the guy mid-leap in one swift roundhouse kick, sending him flying to the floor with a moaning thud. Before Toby could recover and roll away, Reece dove, grabbing him by the shoulders and tossed him over onto his belly.

"Nice rescue," she said from her fabric-encased chair. "I knew you'd come."

"I told you it was my job to rescue you," he said, one knee in the kid's back while he untied what was left of the boa from her hands. The twerp struggled, but Reece had no problem wrenching his arms together and tying them tight with the pink feather rope.

"Cocky," she murmured.

"It's not cocky if the confidence is justified," he reminded her with a grin.

Her smile, painful as it looked, made his heart stutter.

"You listened," she said softly as she watched him roll the trussed creep out of his way.

"Sweetheart," he told her, still on his knees as he pulled her in her chair toward him for a hug. "I promise, I'll always listen to you."

She looked as if she wanted to say more, to ask him something. Reece's heart skipped, his stomach tensing. Then the sound of cops bursting into the studio filled the room.

The moment passed. Reece wanted to kick everyone's asses out, to tell them to arrest the loser later, but he knew he couldn't.

Patience, he thought as he loosed Sierra from the knotted fabrics. He had plenty of patience.

After all, he'd been waiting six years already. He could wait a few more hours.

SIERRA LAY BACK on the cushioned lounge chair, letting the sound of crickets and her small waterfall soothe her. It was hard to believe it'd only been yesterday that Reece had rescued her from Toby. It felt as if years had passed. Probably because she hadn't seen Reece since he'd hauled Toby off with the cops.

A movement by the door caught her eye. Like a wish, there he was. She should have been surprised, but she wasn't.

"I thought you'd be halfway to Kentucky by now," she said, not bothering to hide her pleasure at the sight of him. She was through hiding. That didn't mean she wasn't nervous as hell to hear what he had to say, though.

"I'm stationed here now," he told her, leaning against the doorframe and shoving his hands in his front pockets. He looked like a little boy all grown up, not sure of his reception but determined to try his best.

"You took the job?" she asked. Nerves fell away at his words. Expectation and joy, something she'd never believed she'd have, filled her heart.

"You knew about it? And you didn't say anything?" The look on his face made it clear he didn't know if that was good or bad.

She gave a little shrug. "Yeah, I knew. But it had to be your decision. You had enough years of being manipulated and pushed into doing things for someone else's dreams. I wouldn't ask you to drop yours to be here with me."

"So you were set on goodbye?" His furrowed brow made it clear that he didn't like that answer.

Sierra smirked. "Hardly. I'd already bought a pair of Louboutin cowboy boots."

"You were coming to me?" Shock wiped away the hurt she'd seen in his eyes. Shock and, judging by the smile curving one corner of his mouth, pleasure.

Sierra sucked in a breath, careful of her swollen lip. This was almost as hard as facing down Toby. Either way, she was leaving herself vulnerable. Laying it all out and hoping she could handle the results.

But she'd already proved that she could, hadn't she? Hell yeah, she had. So she just grinned and gave him a saucy wink. "I figured you'd be missing me in a week or so."

His grin was huge. Bright, happy and boyish. As if Christmas morning, popping his cherry and his first car were all tied up in that smile. Joy burst in Sierra's heart, happiness wrapping around her like a comfy blanket.

"I'd love to see you in Kentucky," he mused.

"Well, it sounds like you just blew your chance," she said, reminding him he'd taken the job offer.

"Will you visit there with me?"

Sierra's breath froze, her smile fading as she met his eyes. He wasn't talking about some booty-call vacation. The look on his face said it was so much more. She couldn't answer.

"I want you to meet my dad, the rest of my family," he said. "I mean, you'll meet them all at Mitch's wedding. But maybe afterward, we can take a few weeks, go back and…"

Her smooth-talking cowboy was speechless. Sierra didn't know if it was nerves or emotion. Pushing herself out of her chair, she sauntered across the patio, using the dozen steps to try to gather her thoughts.

But when she reached him, she still didn't know what to say. She linked her fingers together nervously and rubbed her bare toes over the smooth flagstone.

The ball was in her court.

Staring into his eyes, she saw everything she needed, everything she'd never realized she wanted. Strength, humor, daring. He'd push her, she knew. He'd never let her take the easy route or ignore a challenge. He knew her weaknesses and he didn't care about them.

Sierra heaved a long sigh and tilted her head to one side. Yesterday she'd faced down a crazy blackmailing pervert and thought it would be the hardest thing she'd ever do in her life.

And she'd been right. Because this was easy.

"I love you," she said with a smile. "Just thought you might want to know."

He let out a cowboy-worthy whoop, and before she could blink had grabbed her around the waist and swung her in a wide circle. Holding her tight to him, Reece grinned down into her face. His eyes showed concern, but he brushed a gentle kiss over her mouth, his tongue snaking out to soothe the wounded flesh.

"I take it that makes you happy," she teased.

"About as happy as I plan to make you," he promised. "I never thought I'd hear those words from you. I wanted to…so bad. But to be honest, I never thought I was good enough."

Her jaw dropped in shock. "You're kidding, right?"

"Prada," he pointed out.

Sierra shrugged. "I can get my own Prada," she assured him. "I want a guy who makes me want to take it off. Who can look beyond the designer package and wants me anyway."

"I want you," he assured her. Then, pressing her to his chest, he said, "I love you."

Their lips met in a joyful promise. The kiss was all the sweeter for the tenderness of it. The gentle pledge that yes, wild sex rocked, but they had more. Sierra had never expected more. But oh man, she was glad she'd gotten it.

Fifteen minutes, a few dozen kisses and a fun grope or two later, they curled up together in the wicker lounge chair. Sierra sighed, happy contentment filling her.

"Not to burst our bubble here," Reece said, his words muffled against her hair, "but I had a really weird call today from Rose Donovan. Any clue why?"

She waited. But none of the fear came. No worry, no shame, nothing. Sierra grinned. The only thing keeping her from dancing around the yard in joy was how good it felt to be in Reece's arms.

"Did you talk to her?" Sierra asked.

"Nope, just listened to her rambling message. There were a few threats, a few offers, all woven between slurs."

Oops, Aunt Rose had done a drunk bender. Sierra wondered if she could just let it go at that, then realized that Reece deserved the truth. And that she was strong enough to tell him. Trusted him enough to open that door and let him see her past.

So she did. For thirty minutes, with a few tears and even more cusswords from Reece, she shared all the details of her past. The accusations, the fear, the sexual advances. The police derision, the lawsuit, and finally, the bribes she'd made to keep them out of her life. For the first time, she didn't feel shame, just relief.

"She was probably pissed and blames you," she said, finally winding back around to her aunt's phone call. "Actually it's me she's mad at. I rescinded her bribe. I finally realized as long as I refused to face the past and stand up to them, they could terrorize me."

She recalled how powerful she had felt to step free of her aunt's tyrannical hold. Power and faith in herself gave her a whole different perspective. Just because ugly things had happened in her life didn't make her a victim. And neither had she caused any of the ugliness.

"Toby was just the same as my aunt," she explained, leaning her head back to meet his gaze. "After my little feather bondage with Toby, I realized that you can't ignore bullies. Because even if they promise to go away, they're always haunting you. Even if it's only in the back of your own mind."

"I plan on having a talk with your relatives when your uncle gets back into the country," Reece said. He watched her closely, as if he were waiting for an explosion.

She sighed and shook her head. "No."

Disappointment filled his eyes.

"I'm going to have a talk with them," she told him. "You're welcome to come along if you'd like. Be all big and burly and protective. But I have to be the one to do it. Otherwise nothing changes."

"Damn, sweetheart, you are one smart cookie."

Sierra grinned and hugged his waist.

"The client?" Reece asked as he tucked her tighter into his arms. "Did they follow through with their threat to sue?"

Sierra gave a soft laugh, amazed at how good it felt to be held by him, how right. "No, actually they're not."

"I'm surprised."

"I was, too. But after you guys rescued me, Tristan worked his charms. He pointed out to Corinne and company that if she, such an upstanding woman, could be exploited like that, it could happen to anyone. He agreed to help them with a pictorial article on the subject. They're all up in arms and have a new cause now."

She felt Reece's smile against her hair. Then his chest rumbled with laughter. "Leave it to that guy. I've never known anyone quite so…"

"Charming? Persuasive? Charismatic?"

"Self-possessed," he said, talking over her recitation of Tristan's qualities.

Sierra leaned back to meet his eyes and smiled.

"Still jealous?" she teased.

"Nah, I've got the girl."

"You do," she agreed. "The question is, what are you going to do with her?"

"Giddyup," he said.

Sierra laughed, a feeling of freedom and joy filling her. Yeah, life was good once you met it head on. Just like she planned to do from now on, with Reece right here by her side.

In a quick, easy move, she flipped so he was flat on the lounge. She straddled his waist, curved her hands over his shoulders and looked into his calm blue eyes. Yeah. This was her future. And she liked it.

She swiped his hat and put it on her own head. "Ride me, cowboy."

* * * * *

Turn the page for a sneak preview of

Cody

All Miranda Rivers wants is a sexy one-night stand. But when she picks up sexy rodeo star – and vampire – Cody Braddock, that one night might last an eternity…

by Kimberly Raye

Cody
by
Kimberly Raye

Texas, Present Day

HE HADN'T HAD SEX IN forty-eight hours.

While two days of deprivation was nothing for most men, Cody Braddock wasn't the average guy. He was a hell-raising, adrenaline-loving, nine-time Professional Bull Riders champion—known to the world as Cody "Balls to the Wall" Boyd—just weeks away from record-breaking buckle number ten.

He was also a vampire who fed off of blood and sex.

Cody was desperate for both as he walked into the crowded Sixth Street bar in the heart of Austin, Texas.

A Nickelback song blasted from the loudspeakers and vibrated the walls. A splatter of colored lights bounced off the sea of writhing bodies that filled the small dance floor. The air reeked of beer and stale cigarette smoke.

It was the kind of place people came to drown their troubles and forget. A bad day. A cheating spouse. An arrogant boss. A stack of unpaid bills.

A little liquid courage, a lot of sex, and all would be right with the world. Or so they thought.

He read that much in their gazes, and what he couldn't see when he made direct eye contact, he felt.

Lust and desperation swirled into a nearly irresist-ible aphrodisiac that filled his nostrils and lured him deeper inside the club. Body heat pushed and pulled at him from every angle. Dozens of heartbeats mingled together in a steady *ba-bom ba-bom* that echoed in his head and throbbed through his body. A strange aware-ness crawled up his spine and he glanced to the right.

His gaze collided with a pair of deep, unreadable brown eyes and he quickly realized he wasn't the only one looking for a little action tonight.

He didn't know the guy's name or anything about him. He only knew that the young gun wasn't human and that he'd come to feed. A long time ago, Cody would have been surprised at running into another vampire. They'd been few and far between back when Cody had been turned.

But now…

There were more. They existed side-by-side with humans, feeding on them when the need arose and tossing them when they were finished. They were the ultimate predators. Alluring. Persuasive. Powerful. In-vincible. *Deadly.* The moral barometer had slipped away right along with the humanity. Forgotten like a bad day.

For most.

But Cody refused to forget.

He still remembered the last beat of his heart. The last draw of breath. The last flutter of life. The memories haunted him, driving him almost as fiercely as the hunger. To find the vampire who'd slaughtered his family that fateful night and destroy him once and for all.

Cody still had several miles to go before he reached his destination—a small town north of San Antonio, Texas. But he was a hell of a lot closer than he'd been when he'd first seen the copy of *Motorcycle Mania* featuring the trio behind Skull Creek Choppers, the fastest growing custom motorcycle manufacturer in the south.

One glance at the picture and he'd been pulled back to the moment when his life had changed forever. When *he'd* changed. In a fiery blaze, he'd lost everything that mattered to him—his mother, his sister-in-law, his nephew, his brothers, his home.

Not that Brent, Travis and Colton were dead like the others. His brothers had suffered a fate far worse than a mortal death—they'd been turned just as Cody had. They lived in isolation now, feeding off blood and sex, doomed to an eternity of hunger. One eaten up by guilt, one driven by anger, one so indifferent he didn't give a shit about anyone or anything.

And Garret Sawyer, the creative genius behind SCC, was the vampire responsible.

Cody could still remember the pain in his skull, the blackness. When he'd regained consciousness, it had been Sawyer who'd loomed over him, his fangs bared, his face and clothes covered in soot and blood. He'd held a knife in his hand.

The same knife he'd used to kill Cody's mother.

Cody's oldest brother Colton had seen Sawyer, as well. The same face. The blood. The knife.

It was Sawyer, all right. It had to be.

And Cody intended to make him pay for what he'd

done. Maybe then the what-ifs would stop once and for all.

What if he hadn't left his brothers to head for town?

What if he'd ridden in a minute sooner?

What if he'd been there?

Cody forced aside the endless questions and concentrated on the task at hand—feeding and gathering his strength.

He shifted his attention back to the younger vampire. He gave a quick nod. The vamp replied in kind before turning back to the woman next to him. He smiled and the brunette practically swooned. A split second later, he steered her toward the rear exit.

Cody's gut tightened and his mouth watered, and anxiety rushed through him. His shoulder cried, reminding him of yesterday's practice ride on an ornery bull named Mabel prior to picking up the *Motorcycle Mania* issue. While vampires weren't susceptible to mortal injuries, they still felt pain. More so than the average human thanks to heightened senses. Translation—when he hurt, he friggin' *hurt*.

Not for long though.

He stared through the dim interior and met a pair of deep blue eyes rimmed in a quarter inch of black eyeliner.

Her name was Laura and this was the first time she and her new boyfriend had gone out on the town as a couple. She loved the guy who stood next to her with his arm around her waist, but she wished he wouldn't act so damned possessive. It wasn't like she was going to ditch him. Although she might consider it if the hot-looking cowboy staring at her gave the slightest indication that he had the same thing in mind.

The arm tightened around her waist and Cody shifted his gaze to her companion. His name was Mark and he worked on a road crew. He didn't like men looking at his woman and he sure as hell didn't like his woman looking at any men.

Cody tipped his hat and shifted his gaze elsewhere. There were too many available women to get himself stuck in a love triangle. Especially when he wasn't looking for love, or anything close. Not that such a thing existed. He'd been around over one hundred and fifty years and never in all that time had he seen anything close to such an emotion. Like? Yes. Lust? Hell, yes. But one man/one woman, to have and to hold, 'til death do us part *love?*

It just didn't exist. Not for a vampire like Cody, or the man he'd once been.

A man just like his father.

He ignored the thought. It didn't matter now. The only thing that mattered to him was sustenance.

Strength.

Sex.

© Kimberly Groff 2009

CODY & BELOW THE BELT
(2-IN-1 ANTHOLOGY)

BY KIMBERLY RAYE & SARAH MAYBERRY

Cody

When sexy rodeo star – and vampire – Cody Braddock picks Miranda as his mate, their sensual night together could last an eternity...

Below the Belt

Jamie's determined to become a world-class boxer – but she'll need gorgeous trainer Cooper's help. And she'll have to resist his sizzling hot body if she wants to win!

SOLDIER IN CHARGE
BY JENNIFER LaBRECQUE

Smouldering-hot soldier Mitch is a play-by-the-rules kind of guy. Too bad his latest assignment is to protect free-spirited Eden... *who only wants to play with him...*

UNLEASHED
BY LORI BORRILL

Detective Rick needs Jessica to help uncover missing evidence. Yet Jess isn't just the key to unlocking the case. She could release his pent-up passion too!

On sale from 17th September 2010
Don't miss out!

Available at WHSmith, Tesco, ASDA, Eason and all good bookshops

www.millsandboon.co.uk

0910/14

2 FREE BOOKS
AND A SURPRISE GIFT

We would like to take this opportunity to thank you for reading this Mills & Boon® book by offering you the chance to take TWO more specially selected titles from the Blaze® series absolutely FREE! We're also making this offer to introduce you to the benefits of the Mills & Boon® Book Club™—

- **FREE home delivery**
- **FREE gifts and competitions**
- **FREE monthly Newsletter**
- **Exclusive Mills & Boon Book Club offers**
- **Books available before they're in the shops**

Accepting these FREE books and gift places you under no obligation to buy, you may cancel at any time, even after receiving your free books. Simply complete your details below and return the entire page to the address below. You don't even need a stamp!

YES Please send me 2 free Blaze books and a surprise gift. I understand that unless you hear from me, I will receive 3 superb new books every month, including a 2-in-1 book priced at £4.99 and two single books priced at £3.19 each, postage and packing free. I am under no obligation to purchase any books and may cancel my subscription at any time. The free books and gift will be mine to keep in any case.

Ms/Mrs/Miss/Mr_____ Initials _____

Surname _____

Address _____

_____ Postcode _____

E-mail _____

Send this whole page to: Mills & Boon Book Club, Free Book Offer, FREEPOST NAT 10298, Richmond, TW9 1BR